THE RAKE OF TAMARIX HALL

A NOVEL

GEORGINA NORTH

Sarah ♥
Thank you
so much for
coming and being
a supporter from
day 1 !! love you ♥
♥georgina♥
1.28.2023

PEPPERBERRY PRESS

THE RAKE OF TAMARIX HALL | Copyright © 2022 by Georgina North

Library of Congress Cataloging-in-Publication Data

Names: North, Georgina, author.
Title: The Rake of Tamarix Hall: A Novel / Georgina North.
Description: First U.S. edition | San Diego: Pepperberry Press, 2023.

Identifiers: LCCN 2022922140 (print) | ISBN 978-1-959794-01-1 (paperback) ISBN 978-1-959794-00-4 (hardcover) | ISBN 978-1-959794-02-8 (ebook)

Cover design by Robin Vuchnich

For the girl at the yellow table

'*Y*our uncle is dead.'

Words designed to shock others failed to elicit even an uninterested glance from Lucius Anselme, contented bachelor, well-known rake, eldest son of the late Mr and Mrs Anselme—and, with the death of his grand-uncle Gervais Heaston, the reluctant new Marquess of Windmere.

'Well?' His aunt Bea pinned him with her stare, her eyes the same unique blue-green as his own, the unusual colour not unlike the calm waters of the Adriatic Sea. She had delivered the news with little fanfare but seemed to anticipate—nay, desire—a greater reaction than that with which it was received.

'Well what, Aunt?'

'You have nothing to say?'

'Perhaps you have enough for us both.' Lucius finally looked up from his seat behind the large desk of his study, long enough only to raise one challenging eyebrow, intent as he was on completing the letter in front of him. It was a short note, really, with nothing more than a time and desired attire (none), to be sent to his current Cyprian, a black-haired beauty with a body that just begged to be touched.

'Don't be smart with me, Lucius.'

He sighed, pulled at a stray lock the rich, deep brown of dark tobacco, and relented. 'I'd rather it was someone else having this conversation. That would mean it was someone else's responsibility. I've already more than enough for one man.'

On the death of his father, a little more than a decade ago when he was just two-and-twenty, Lucius inherited his family's four-thousand-acre estate, a cottage in Cornwall, a château on the southern coast of France, and the Anselme lace empire. The remote possibility of becoming marquess had always existed, but as Lucius had no need and even less desire for a title, funds, or a connection to that line of the family, he had given the possibility as much consideration in his youth as he did now—which is to say, nearly none at all.

'It would likely feel so when you spend as much time collecting highflyers as tending to your duties.'

'My duties include providing occupation to those wanting. Shall I tell you what Lady Colchester wants, aside from an apology for being thought a Cyprian?' he asked, with his infuriatingly charming smile.

'You are a shocking, brazen-faced boy, Lucius. Why I continue to subject myself to your crass, teasing manners…'

Lucius smiled, genuinely this time, as he came around the desk and placed a kiss on her cheek before settling himself in the chair next to the one where she perched. 'Come now, ma'am, you can't gammon me. You've heard far worse from your own cronies than anything I've ever said.'

She sniffed.

'You wished to astonish me with your news, and I disappointed those hopes. Can you possibly forgive me? It's all the solicitor's fault, truly. He sent an express while the body was still warm. Ah, and now I can tell you're furious with me for being in possession of this information and withholding it.' Lucius was teasing his aunt, but the truth was he wanted to sit with the news, the inevitable changes to his life, in the peace and quiet of his own mind before contending with his aunt, his brother, and any other person with a feeling or opinion on the matter, which was likely to be everyone as soon as the notice of his grand-uncle's death came out in the papers—another responsibility that fell to him as the new marquess.

'Will it put me back in your good graces to know I've already started the process of deeding Branford Park to Alexander?' The only person in the world Lucius cared about as much as he cared about himself was his younger brother, and being able to give him their childhood home was the only positive outcome of the situation. 'He certainly deserves it, and then perhaps he and Miss Dench will find their way back to one another. What need have I for Branford now that I've Tamarix Hall and however many more?'

'You have not seen the solicitor, then?'

'No, although I wrote of my plans to remain in town for another fortnight, busy as I am collecting my ladybirds.'

'Lucius,' his aunt scolded.

'No need for the sour face. I've only the one, and I'm giving her a lovely ruby necklace this evening as a parting gift.' When his aunt's face remained pinched and disbelieving, he added, 'I imagine I'll be at Tamarix some months. There's no reason she ought to wait for me to return. In fact, I'd prefer she did not. She's becoming too attached by half.'

'Her husband's a dolt.'

'Her husband busies himself with an opera dancer. Nevertheless, it would be best for her to find a new lover if that's what she wishes.'

'You as well.'

His eyes hardened. 'No.'

'You've no choice in the matter now.'

'Are you going to strap me to the bed and throw an eligible miss on top of me?'

A cat-like smile stretched across Aunt Bea's face, her features still shockingly youthful for a woman on the wrong side of sixty, in stark contrast to her hair, which had gone white when Lucius was still a youth. 'If I have to.'

Despite her small frame and the deceptive air of fragility that came with age, he knew she was still quite capable of seeing through any scheme to which she devoted herself.

'Anything but that, Aunt, I beg of you. There is nothing so boring as a gently bred young lady.' He shuddered as the words rolled out.

'You'll need an heir, Lucius, particularly now that you've the title.'

'No.'

'Lucius, really.' His aunt let out an impatient sigh. 'You're no better than a recalcitrant child. Find some diamond, beget an heir, and go back to your ways.'

'Diamond is an apt name for those young ladies. Sparkling on the outside, nothing within. A ladybird would be a much more interesting choice, no?' He pressed his lips together to keep from smiling when his aunt's eyes briefly narrowed in annoyance. 'It seems if that's the option, you'd rather I not marry at all. I'm quite in agreement, ma'am. Matrimony has never been palatable for me.'

'Don't be ridiculous. You're a marquess now, and even

before that'—she shook her head in irritation—'you knew what was expected of your position. More to the point, you've had three years to accustom yourself to this version of your future.'

'How snobbish you sound.' Lucius was mostly jesting, but his aunt felt her consequence and liked when others felt it too. He also had no rebuttal, because his aunt was right. It had been several years since he received a letter from a Mr Adams, one of the solicitors for the previous marquess, informing Lucius that he was the marquess's heir, after his second cousin, James Heaston, better known as Viscount Torring, had died in a riding accident.

For three years, Lucius had done little else but pray for some other relation to appear and contest his claim. Inheriting from his grand-uncle meant taking on the seven thousand acres of Tamarix situated in the gently rolling hills of Berkshire, a handful of smaller estates, a hunting lodge in Scotland, however many more tenants and staff, and a seat in the House of Lords—the latter perhaps the only thing he found any interest in.

'There's that redheaded girl coming out this season, the Parkers' eldest daughter. Quite the dowry, I'm told, and if she's anything like her mother, won't care in the least what you do after you're wed.'

'Charming.' Lucius was aware of his reputation—and aware that the rest of the *ton* was too—although he thought 'rake' a tad excessive. He liked learning a woman's body, the things that would bring her the most pleasure, conquering her darkest desires, and then when he got bored, he moved on to the next. But he never dallied with or ruined innocent young ladies; he preferred widows and, on occasion, an unhappily married wife, like Lady Colchester. They were already broken in, ready to please and be pleased, and without the risk of compromise.

His aunt looked at him with the same kind of gleam in her eyes as when she planned her fatal attack on the chessboard, and he could see the words forming in her mouth before she even said them. 'And should something happen to you? Alexander has no desire and less aptitude to be a marquess. It would be his undoing.'

Lucius frowned at the truth of this statement. His younger brother had always been the exception to the rule—happy to be the younger son and content with a simpler life. He studied law and worked for a solicitor in London. He was intelligent but had no interest in becoming a barrister; Alexander disliked speaking in front of an audience almost as much as he disliked arguing of any kind. Although the younger Anselme was capable enough of managing Branford Park, particularly as Lucius had ensured their childhood home could very nearly run itself, Alexander had stated, unequivocally and on more than one occasion, that he was relieved to be born second.

'Aunt Bea, now that I'm a marquess, I feel it's entirely within my bounds to demand you not always be so sensible. It's a trifle irritating.'

She matched his sarcasm when she answered. 'Come now, you still have your Aunt Margot. One can only imagine the letter that ninny will send—a packet of pages, lines crossed every which way, and not an intelligent thought to be had.'

'Of that I have no doubt. I can only account for the differences in your characters by supposing as the eldest you got all the sense, and there was none left by the time she came round. It will interest you to know, though, that a letter turned up this morning from Lady Lisle.'

Aunt Bea raised both brows in surprise. 'Well, she's not a woman to waste time.'

'I suppose with both her husband and son too dead to ascend to the title, and sadly for us both no other heir forthcoming, she's finally begun to revise her stratagems for keeping some connection to Tamarix.'

'With two unmarried daughters, the greatest surprise is that she did not present her whole person, dragging those ninnyhammers in her wake. No, I reclaim that statement. The greatest surprise is that she waited until the old man died to begin her campaign.'

'Indeed, ma'am.' Lucius had seen Lady Lisle from time to time while in town, and his opinion was both strong and firmly fixed: she was conceited, rude, and would not be welcome in half the drawing rooms in which she was often present if not for her family's ancient lineage. The only common ground they shared, until now, was their equal desire to maintain the rift in the family.

His great-grandfather Heaston had had numerous offspring, including two boys, the younger being Lucius's grandfather, Silas. With everything destined for the elder, Silas Heaston was lucky enough to fall in love with a French heiress, but her fortune came from trade, and when he married against the will of his family, he was cast off.

Lucius had been blessed to know his grandfather and grandmother a little bit in his younger years, and there was never a moment as far as he could tell that either regretted their decision or the divide it caused in the family. With her dowry, Silas purchased Branford Park, and he took his wife's name, Anselme, not only to cast off the most tangible connection to those who had abandoned him, but to honour his father-in-law, who had taught Silas everything there was to know about lace-making and left the centuries-old family business in his capable hands.

The joke was now on his great-grandfather, Lucius thought, as he retrieved the letter from Lady Lisle to share with his Aunt Bea.

'Oh, the presumption.' The older lady guffawed as she read through the lines of the letter. 'If I was unable to appreciate the folly in others, I might choose to take offence at her nerve. Such as it is, I daresay we are in for quite a treat now that she is determined to establish some kind of connection. How long until she appears in the drawing room at Tamarix? No doubt she still possesses some friends in that neighbourhood—at least one would think so after living above twenty years there. Thank goodness for small blessings, I suppose. Had her husband had enough sense to stay alive until he could inherit, she would have rights to the dower house.'

Lucius lifted one dark, straight eyebrow, a perfect note of censure, in his aunt's direction.

'Pah! I said it, but you were thinking it.'

'Yes, but *you* said it,' he returned with a laugh. A thoughtful silence settled between them. 'I'm thinking I'll perhaps ask Alexander to accompany me when I venture to Tamarix. When I saw him yesterday...' Lucius trailed off, unsure how exactly he wanted to finish that sentence.

'The break will do him good before he takes over the reins of Branford, and fresh air is known to cure all manner of ills.'

'You, too, have noticed he seems not quite his usual self?'

Aunt Bea's eyes were sharp, penetrating, but all she said was, 'I've my suspicions.'

'Any you care to share?'

'None. You'll either agree with me and take credit for the insight or disagree, as if there's any possibility of my being wrong. Take him—a little adventure won't do him harm at any rate.'

'THERE's something I've longed to ask you, brother,' Alexander said, as their horses trotted down the country lane. The pair were approaching Frambury, the market town near Tamarix that was surrounded by quaint villages, country manors, and charming cottages covered in leafless vines and edged in by hedgerows running this way and that.

'How unlike you to restrain yourself. What's that?'

'Is that mark on your cheek from some freak shaving accident—although there was never so steady a hand as your man's—or did the ruby fail to placate Lady Colchester?'

There was no one, Lucius thought privately, able to feign artlessness quite like his own brother. 'Come closer, Alexander, so I may toss you off your mount.' Alexander's laughter rippled the air around them. 'I managed to dodge the vase but not the comb. It's my own fault, perhaps, for not ending it sooner—or perhaps hers for marrying a man older than even her own grandpapa in the first place. Naturally one would prefer the scandal of eloping to being tupped by the old toast to whom she's yoked herself.'

Alexander, who had yanked on his reins in surprise, causing his horse to throw its head, exclaimed, 'She never!'

'Had I failed to mention that? She's been hinting for some time now, and after the comb found its mark, she begged my pardon and pleaded with me to take her to Italy.'

'Hasn't she children?'

'Three, as a matter of fact. She was labouring, it seems, under the misapprehension that once she satisfactorily fulfilled that duty, her lord would cease his amorous attentions, which, she informed me, were intolerable, and she said if I held her in any affection, I would release her from such repulsive drudgery. Her words, not mine.'

After a moment, Alexander said, with more contemplation than the words warranted, 'You are known to enjoy a passionate woman.'

'Passionate, yes. Deluded, no.'

'You're likely the only man ever to refuse her something she wanted. I still remember when she was Miss Digby. There wasn't an eye that didn't turn her way wherever she went. I can't say I wasn't shocked when I read that she'd chosen Lord Colchester from her pack of suitors.'

'Mr Digby was under the hatches and owed a number of people fairly significant sums.'

'I thought she'd a dowry of twenty thousand?'

'You and every one of her young beaux. The problem with young beaux, of course, is that they almost never have much to offer.'

'I'm well aware.' Alexander's voice was more cynical than bitter. Lucius turned to him with a chiding look. 'Yes, I know, I know. I've never been one of those young men—and now I never will be, thanks to Branford. Even if I was, it's not as if you conspired to be born first. Besides,' Alexander offered with a sheepish smile, 'I'd be bloody awful as a marquess. Can you imagine me in the House of Lords?' He gave an exaggerated shudder.

'You could do it if needs must.'

'You mean if you continue without a legitimate heir?'

'I've no *illegitimate* ones, either, I'll thank you to remember.'

'Luci.' Alexander grew serious. 'For all I've said—and

meant—that I'm quite happy to be second, you need not do anything on my behalf you find repugnant.'

'In that case, you'll be kind enough to return Branford Park.'

Lucius knew Alexander would try his best, might even make a half-decent go of it, if he had to become marquess. He also knew the pressure, the expectations, the responsibilities, and any number of things that attended his new role would make his brother miserable, in part because it was unasked for and unwanted. Lucius knew that feeling well; he hadn't wished to leave school at seventeen to care for his mama, he hadn't asked to take over running Branford at twenty when his own father could do so no longer, he had no desire to be a marquess—but he always accepted the duties set out before him. Lucius had carried more so that as a child, Alexander wasn't the one cleaning up clumps of their mother's hair; so that as a youth, he could be away at Eton and then Oxford; so that as a young man, he could spend his time how and with whom he wished.

The pair fell into silence as they made their way toward Frambury.

There was no mistaking their connection. The Anselme brothers were taller than average, broad shouldered, and in possession of the same angular jaw and sharp cheekbones, defined by the little hollows under them. Their lips were a touch full, the upper one rising to two prominent peaks, and Lucius's hair was several shades darker, but both men had unruly waves that fell with an unfair natural precision other gentlemen spent hours trying to recreate.

They were similar in looks rather than personality. Lucius enjoyed company, flirting, and parties; he went to town every season; and he had long become accustomed to attention, to being hunted by matchmaking mamas and young ladies who thought they might hold the key to his heart, or at the very least his purse strings. Alexander preferred the intimacy of small gatherings where he knew everyone, lived in London but attended events only when Lucius compelled him, and had romantic notions about love and marriage entirely at odds with his elder brother's.

Lucius turned away to hide a sigh as he contemplated the two options now before him, neither of which he cared for. He must either consign himself to a life he didn't want by marrying and having an heir, or he must consign his beloved brother to a life entirely unsuited to his abilities and desires. Both made Lucius's stomach turn.

'SOPHIA HEARD from one of the maids that the new marquess is to arrive Thursday—a cousin or something of the sort to the previous one.'

Lucius rolled his eyes as the hushed feminine voice wafted from the next row over. He had stopped in the Frambury bookshop while Alexander went in search of a blacksmith or farrier who could reshoe his horse before they continued on to Tamarix. As a rule, Lucius thought nothing of country gossip or the silly ladies who propagated it, but his hand stalled as he reached for a book when he heard the reply.

'Will we be expected to bow and scrape to him just like the last? If so, I'd much rather he stay away—or turn the house into a school, or a home for young ladies who find themselves uncomfortably circumstanced.' This voice had a similar tone and lilt, but unlike the first it was filled with disgust.

'You're being outrageous, and I won't allow you to provoke me.'

'I am not. What good have those people ever done? Spare me from ever encountering another Heaston, and I'll love you longer than forever.'

Lucius couldn't decide if he was amused, in agreement, affronted, or a bit of all three.

'*Those* people? You mean the people who provide livelihoods and homes and charity for our neighbours?'

'Old Marquess Windmere was one of the worst people to tread upon English soil. The Yateses worked for him for years, and he left them with hardly six pennies to scrape together. And the rest of that odious family—' The girl broke off with such anger Lucius's head snapped back.

'Cressida.' The name was said in that half-chiding, half-exasperated way only ever mastered by one's family.

Cressida. He silently rolled the name around in his mouth. He hadn't meant to eavesdrop. In fact, he hadn't even realised there were other people in the bookshop besides himself.

'How can you of all people defend them?'

'I'm not defending *them*. I am defending *him*, this man whom we have yet to meet.'

Lucius walked to the end of the row and turned the corner, prepared to lay eyes on a hoyden and an angel, only to find it empty. He looked down the next to no avail before hearing familiar voices coming from the front of the shop. As he approached to take his place in the queue, he noted that the ladies were of a similar height, coming to about his shoulder, and shared the same lithe build, but one had rich brown hair like his own and the other had locks in the palest shade of gold, like a cold glass of champagne.

When the owner mentioned Miss Cressida by name, Lucius

noted she was the one with the pale hair. He waited for them to finish and turn around, wondering if the fractious girl would have some mark upon her person—a squat nose, an unsightly scar—declaring her as rotten outside as in.

It was at that moment the ladies spun about, and Lucius felt himself knocked backwards by the brilliant laurel-green eyes looking right at him. There was a translucence about them, as if light was shining from within, and Lucius discovered he was, in an unusual turn, wordless.

Miss Cressida opened her mouth as if to say something, but the girl with her spoke up first in her gentle voice, begged his pardon, and swept past him without a second glance. He watched their retreating figures a moment, still contemplating her fine eyes and how her bottom lip was a little fuller than the top, but both perfectly peach in colour, before stepping up to the counter.

'They're taking young ladies. It's a shame their father won't let them spread their wings a little,' the bookshop owner said.

'I beg your pardon?'

'The Misses Ambrose. Your mouth is hanging open and your eyes agog. I don't blame you, young man, and don't think you'll pull the wool over my eyes if you say otherwise.'

Lucius felt a lazy smile tug at the corner of his mouth. He was approaching his thirty-third year.

'There's two more, too, down the lane at Red Fern Grange, but I'd go on as if I didn't know that if I were you.'

'Why should I ever do such a silly thing?'

'The girls are all that's good, but they didn't get it from their father. That's all I'll say, and even that's already too much.'

Lucius was still considering those words when he crossed paths with the pair once more as they came out of the milliner's. Their heads had been huddled together as they squeezed through the shop door side by side, and whatever it was they were discussing was enough to pull their attention from the walkway in front of them. He nearly knocked the two over, steadying a shoulder of each with his hands.

'It seems we'll spend our day begging your pardon, sir,' commented the brown-haired girl as she righted herself.

'For my part, I can think of worse ways to spend a day,' he said, with a grin that was as inviting as it was heart stopping.

'Doing it a bit brown, sir, do not you think?' Miss Cressida challenged, seemingly unaffected by his charm.

'Ah, but isn't there something about anonymity that makes us all a little presumptuous? It's much easier to say things about people we've yet to meet than about those already numbered among our acquaintance, is it not?'

Her eyes narrowed. *The termagant is no one's fool.*

'Familiarity is not always necessary to form an opinion.'

'No, but more often than not, it's helpful in forming an accurate one. Allow me to illustrate my point. Without knowing you, I might assume you only read novels and prefer gossip to intellectual conversation.'

The lady's sister, who had the slightly panicked face of one averse to disagreements or confrontations of any sort, put a hand on Miss Cressida's forearm, no doubt hoping to clip the conversation. The attempt was unsuccessful.

'As you are full of insights, perhaps you will share with me your thoughts on gentlemen who listen to conversations to which they have not been invited and can have no part?'

'I would say some discussions are better had in the confines of one's own home.'

'And I would say a true gentleman would announce his presence to prevent further mortification to either party.'

Lucius had closed some of the space he first put between them, but his reply died in his mouth when he became distracted by the smattering of barely there freckles across the bridge of her nose and cheeks.

'Cressida, it's past time for us to be home. Sir.' The other girl dropped a quick curtsey, effectively ending the tête-à-tete. Miss Cressida only deigned to bow her head, pinched her eyes at him once more, and walked away, as if she had nowhere else to be.

2

*C*ressida Ambrose was several months shy of twenty-one, had no prospects, viscerally disliked the most handsome man she'd ever seen, and hoped with every inch of her tall frame that he was watching her walk away but would never look back to discern the truth of the matter.

'The Hobbses are expecting some guests,' her sister Astrid said, knocking one of her shoulders into Cressida's as they wandered from the milliner's, trying to turn that young lady's attention away from their unexpected encounter.

Cressida made no reply, except to murmur, 'Despicable man,' under her breath, and then, turning towards her sister, added in a passion, 'To be set down by some eavesdropping gentleman—nay, a stranger, for we cannot be certain he deserves better than that—who considers us no better than local gossipmongers. How dare he!'

'Well—' Astrid began, pausing only as her sister levelled a glare in her direction, 'we were doing no less than he pointed out. Although I daresay no harm will come from the exchange.

He was dressed for travel and therefore likely passing through.'

An exasperated huff escaped Cressida. 'With my luck, he's very likely to number among the Hobbses' guests. Some eligible brother or cousin, no doubt.'

'Since when do you care a fig about eligible gentlemen?'

She didn't. Cressida hadn't looked at a man in years other than to catalogue his faults and cast judgment. That's when she had her first, only, and worst experience with a suitor—a term she wasn't sure was entirely suitable, as the suiting was all on his side and he was, when all things were considered, a scoundrel masquerading as a gentleman.

'I care when I have the dearest sisters in the world to see comfortably settled, and now I've ruined your chances—not that I'd care to see you wed to someone so detestable, but as the only way we meet new people is while we are in town, I suppose I ought to take more care to guard my tongue.'

'The first part of that speech sounds perilously close to hope,' Astrid joked, but she followed it with a sigh. 'Circumstanced as we are, we must hold close to hope or whatever we can claim near enough to it.'

'Your hope is indefatigable, and it's one of your most charming characteristics. It also falls to my lot then to temper it.'

'What do young ladies like us have if not stores of hope?'

Cressida had heard her sister offer some iteration of that rhetorical question time and again. At three-and-twenty, Astrid's best years were quickly slipping out from under her.

'*You* have an estate.'

'*We* have an estate, if you can call it that. What it will be when it eventually comes to me...' Neither sister needed to speak aloud the end of that sentence. It was a lucky turn for the Ambrose girls that it was their mama who brought the estate to the marriage and their mama's long-gone father who saw that it would go to the eldest daughter if there were no male heirs. Red Fern Grange would go to Astrid upon their father's death, and she could keep all her sisters there with her. But despite the potential of a relatively comfortable income, under their father's lazy management the estate struggled to produce enough to cover the necessities for the four girls in the family and wouldn't do so at all without the little bit of economy Astrid was able to employ. They often browsed in Mr Taff's bookshop, but they rarely made a purchase.

'Then *we'll* figure it out when the time comes,' Cressida said, linking arms with her sister.

'We won't have much of a choice. Perhaps with a little hard work and quite a bit of scrimping, we'll be able to give the younger girls a season of sorts, although I never received a return letter from Aunt Delia, and I'm unsure who else we could put upon for such a thing.'

'The only way any of that can matter is if Father is kind enough to kick over sooner than later, and he's never done a kind thing in his life.'

Even that was too kind a way to phrase it. Mr Ambrose was a hard, rough man who had been disappointed in his wife and took it out on his daughters, particularly Cressida, for reasons known only to her mother when she'd been alive, and to Cressida herself, who bore it all with an inner strength bolstered by a deep desire to protect her sisters.

Astrid, Cressida often thought, was too gentle for this world, not unlike their mama, and the other two girls were young enough to still need someone else to rely on. In no realm could Cressida imagine subjecting her sisters to more of their father's displeasure simply to lessen her own share. As it was, Mr Ambrose had been drinking himself to an early grave for almost as long as she could remember, and more days than not, he was too incoherent to do much beyond stamping about the house, occasionally throwing things that never hit the intended target, and raising his hollow, slurred voice before passing out in his study.

After a heavy, quiet moment, Astrid asked, 'Should we talk more of that dashing stranger?'

He *was* dashing, dangerously so, and Cressida recalled how she'd peeked back over her shoulder as they left the bookshop, desperate for one more glimpse of that noble mein, the sculpted cheekbones, the strong jaw, that she could stow away in her memories. When they'd run into him again, she'd been as mesmerised by his deep, rolling voice as she'd been provoked by his comments.

'Dashing as he was rude. Who is he to eavesdrop, to insert himself into our business?'

'He was right. We should not have been speaking so in a public place.'

'Mr Taff's shop is hardly a public place.'

'You say so just to be contrary.'

Cressida grinned at her sister. 'Fine. We should not have been speaking so, but it would not have mattered had he not been listening as he was. Oh!' She pulled up short and looked about her person.

'What is it?'

'I must've left the length of green ribbon at the milliner's.' Ribbon was one of the few inexpensive ways they could dress up sad hats and old, reworked dresses. And like her new book, it was to be treasured.

'Let us return then.'

'No,' Cressida said, putting a hand on her sister's arm. 'You remain where you are. You made a valiant effort, but I noticed you hobbling a little.'

Astrid's brows pulled together in consternation. 'There's a pebble in my shoe.'

'After we make the turn, you may safely remove it. For now, we've not gone so far as to lose sight of one another if I go alone—and it could hardly matter if I did,' Cressida added. The Ambrose sisters, having grown up only a mile or so from Frambury, knew almost everyone from the town and the surrounding villages.

'Go on, then.' Astrid made a shooing motion with her hands, and Cressida took off at a pace not quite sedate enough to be ladylike.

The milliner smiled at Cressida and held out the ribbon as soon as she entered.

'Thank you, Mrs Wade. What good is a bonnet if I've not the ribbon with which to trim it?'

Cressida stepped from the shop once again and could see her sister at the other end of the road, new book unfolded in her hands.

'My lucky day, Miss Cressida.'

She started at the voice, the one that had been intruding on her thoughts since she'd last heard it, and looked over to find the man from earlier leaning against the wall of the baker's in the middle of tearing off a chunk of fresh-baked bread.

'What powers you must possess, sir, to know my name when we've not been introduced.'

'Lucius Anselme. The pleasure is entirely mine.' He smirked and lifted one lazy shoulder before executing a perfect sweeping bow.

Cressida bit back several scathing retorts. 'Are you to patronise every shop in Frambury today, sir?'

'I've skipped the milliner, although now I wish I had not.'

'You may not feel bound to behave with any propriety, as evidenced by your earlier eavesdropping,' she flung at him, with as much conceit as a young lady from the country could muster, excising her own wanting behaviour neatly from her mind, 'but I do, and therefore will refrain from telling you how insufferable you are.'

'And yet—'

Cressida watched his smile unfold slowly, as if he knew how she desired a glimpse and took joy in withholding its full effect.

'I've not seen you here before, so I can only assume whatever business you have in Frambury cannot be of any duration. I will wish you well and hope it concludes with all expediency so you may depart as quickly as you came.'

A secretive gleam flickered in his eyes, unsettling her from the inside out. Every nerve ending, ever follicle, every muscle and bone and stretch of sinew holding her together howled at her to run far and fast away from this man, this Hades who would pull her to the underworld before she realised where she was.

'Mr Anselme, I bid you a good day.'

'Miss Cressida,' he purred and bowed low as she moved past him towards her sister, who had let her book fall to her side and was watching the exchange, the concern in her features noticeable even at a distance.

Cressida tried to maintain a calm pace as she went away, but her veins were pulsating, and the effect was that her whole body tremored ever so slightly. When she caught up with Astrid, she grabbed her sister by the elbow with enough force to elicit a little yelp and dragged them to the turn in the road, where they would no longer be visible to anyone on the main lane.

'Cressie! Cressida!' Astrid wrenched her arm free. 'The rock in my shoe.'

'Oh.' Cressida felt and sounded a little out of breath. The queer look her sister gave her meant she heard it too. 'I'm sorry, dearest. I think we are safe here, if you'd like to undo your laces.'

'I don't think you're safe at all,' replied Astrid with typical placidity as she worked the tiny stone out of her shoe.

Cressida was spared the necessity of replying by the arrival of Sophia Harland, daughter of the local rector and close confidante of the eldest Ambrose sisters.

'Just the sisters I was coming to see!' cried Sophia as she emerged from a small copse of trees and approached the pair halted on the side of the quiet lane.

Cressida held out her hands to her friend. 'Yes, what luck that we must always be walking in the same fields and along the same roads. 'Tis almost as if we're neighbours,' she added with a wink.

Ignoring her friend, Sophia retrieved a scrap of newspaper from the reticule dangling from her wrist and unfolded it. 'Listen to this,' she said, her voice quivering with excitement. 'The newly appointed L.W. has flown the coop of his latest ladybird, leaving the raven-haired and sweet-beaked beauty quite put out, if our sources are to be believed. Or perhaps that lady's reported fit of pique has more to do with the striking widow recently seen on his arm at the opera.'

Sophia, whose smile was saucier than any rector's daughter's smile ought to be, looked at the Ambrose sisters with expectant eyes and was not disappointed by Astrid's, 'Goodness.'

'It's hardly worse than everything else we've heard about the man. It is rather interesting, though. When I was in the kitchen the other day trying for a slice of cake, I overheard Cook say one of the larger cottages on the estate is already being refurbished, presumably for his mistress.'

Astrid gasped. 'He would never!'

'It would be rather brazen,' conceded Sophia, after which she suggested the article still clutched in her hand said nothing so bad about the man known only to them through the bits of gossip that travelled through their small part of the country. 'You know, I recall reading about him in the papers quite a bit, only I didn't give it much attention, as I'd not realised he was the heir. But if I recall correctly, he only dallies with widows and married ladies—never an innocent miss.'

'Well,' Cressida replied, in a tone rife with sarcasm, 'that's something, I suppose.'

'You treat the statement with disdain, but it is something, whether you see it as such or not.' When her friend made no further reply, Sophia pressed her point. 'He's a rake with a moral compass, at least.'

'Or he simply hasn't been caught out yet. To men like him, rules that govern most gentlemen are for breaking, not following.'

'You have your opinion. I have mine, and I think his reputation is exaggerated. If he's truly been with half of London, it's not the maidenly half.'

'Sophia!' gasped Astrid, but the other young woman merely turned a level stare on her friend.

'You may rest easy, Astrid. It seems most of the town is inclined to stand on the same side as Cressie here, although I doubt such trenchant and wrong opinions will stand when faced with the man himself.'

Cressida side-eyed her friend. 'Why is that?'

'Because,' Sophia pulled a sly grin, 'what man could bed half of London if he wasn't as charming as he is handsome?'

The three ladies burst into giggles fit for the schoolroom.

'Now, knowing your fixed opinion of this poor man—'

'Poor man! Pah! You've already made him into some kind of hero from a novel.'

'Is he not a rather romantic figure?' Sophia asked with a heady sigh. 'A gentleman thrust into a new place, elevated almost beyond possibility, rumours abounding. Soon we'll hear of a ghost in the tower and some tragic past that holds him hostage.'

'Hostage from what?'

'Anything. Everything. But true love, obviously.'

'Tamarix Hall has no towers.'

Both Cressida and Sophia looked towards Astrid who merely added, 'Well, it does not.'

'Yes, well.' Sophia waved away her friend's logical statement. 'The point is this: there are now two options before you both. You may keep your cheek and your *sound thinking*,' said with a lofty look at the eldest Ambrose, 'or you may hear the latest news.'

Like Sophia, Mrs Harland had the kind of open face and easy manners that made people want to confide in her. As such, the rector's wife was a receptacle for all parish gossip, which she shared with Sophia, who in turn always told Cressida and Astrid.

'We may send her a little bit ahead and you may tell me the news.' Astrid laughed. 'She is quite determined in her ways today.'

'That would only bring out the prickliness in my already

poor character. I beg for your mercy, and the news. Out with it!'

Sophia cast a glance around, as if anyone might be within a mile of them. 'You know I told you that the arrival of the new marquess was imminent.' Both Ambrose sisters nodded. 'Well, he's already in Frambury.' She waited as if to gauge the reactions of her companions.

Astrid offered an interested 'Oh?' but Cressida asked, 'Which half of town was right?' drawing amused looks from her sister and friend.

It was common knowledge by now that the residents of Frambury and its surrounding villages were split in their ideas and notions of the man, with half the population thinking the new marquess would be just as bad or worse than the previous one, and the other half calling that an impossibility, since no one could be as bad. In both halves existed a further divide where his London exploits were concerned. The former marquess had been gruff and reclusive, so much so that reports of his behaviour had over time largely become apocryphal, although there were credible stories from the servants employed at Tamarix and the residents old enough to remember the ungenerous man from the rare occasions he had deigned to appear with his children at a dinner party or assembly.

'That I cannot say just yet,' Sophia said. 'What I can report is this: he's tall, fashionable, amiable, of marrying age, and presumed single since the mistress's rooms weren't prepared at Tamarix, and...' Sophia drew out the word before pausing with dramatic effect.

Cressida laughed. 'You are wasted as a rector's daughter.',

'I'm quite in agreement,' replied Sophia before coming to the climax of her story. 'And,' she said, taking a moment to flick her gaze between the sisters, 'if Mrs Taff is to be believed, so murderously handsome you're likely to need smelling salts just from laying your eyes upon his person.'

'Mrs Taff?' Astrid asked, before Cressida could.

Sophia nodded. 'She was on her way to deliver some books for Papa, but Mama and I came upon her first. She had just seen him, and I think was too full of excitement to do anything but carry her newfound knowledge *somewhere*. And you know people never feel like they're gossiping when they tell all to a rector's wife.'

'Mrs Taff just saw him?' asked Cressida, in fainting accents.

'Yes. He was in the shop this very morning. I'm surprised you didn't see him on the high street. Mrs Taff must've set out as soon as he left,' Sophia added with a wide, laughing smile. 'What? What have I said?'

Astrid was trying and failing to cover her own amusement with a delicate cough. 'Nothing to put you in the fidgets. You've only splashed cold water on Cressie.'

Cressida glared at her sister. 'Nothing of the sort,' she said, denying the claim even as she pictured the roguish quirk of his mouth and quickly reminded herself of his infuriating manners. 'We may have crossed paths with him while at the bookshop.'

'By that, she means we most certainly did,' corrected her sister.

'Did you find him as described?'

Astrid answered first. 'I daresay, and more. When he's not smiling, he looks quite forbidding—or perhaps it's smouldering, like the embers of a dying fire.'

'Astrid is too kind to say a bad word about anybody,' chimed Cressida. 'Conceivably he can be amiable where he chooses, but I found him vexatious, meddlesome, and entirely devoid of manners and charm. Let us have done discussing the rake of Tamarix Hall.' She was too busy kicking stones along the road and watching the paths they cut to notice her sister and friend exchange amused looks.

'What terrible luck, to be sure,' Sophia began—her melodic voice made it easy to miss the sarcasm if one was not acquainted with her—'learning the intolerable man is the new marquess.'

'Of course that man is the new marquess. I should have guessed from his impudence and his complete disposal of propriety that he's a Heaston.' The name was bitter on Cressida's lips. She shook her head to pull herself from the unpleasant memories that fogged her brain whenever she dwelled a moment too long on the past and said in as teasing a voice as she could at that moment muster, 'If I ever want to do you a bad turn, Sophia, I'll simply tell your father what a teasing, artful child you turned out to be.'

Astrid and Sophia carried on as the trio walked towards Red Fern Grange, which was separated from the rectory by an undulating and ill-cared-for field on the southern side of the property, but Cressida couldn't catch on to the conversation. She was wondering why Lord Windmere had introduced himself as Mr Anselme and added liar to the growing list of his faults. She was also wading through a confusing muddle of conflicting feelings: her visceral reaction to this man and competing desires to know him and to see him go away; her concern he would be just the same as the previous heir—everything charming till he was denied what he wanted; the gossip Sophia shared and the twinge of something inside when she thought on it; her disgust with herself and her own behaviour, which she unconsciously managed by assigning those feelings to him rather than herself.

3

'*A*lready charming the locals, are we?' Alexander asked as he strode up to Lucius, who was still watching the young lady drift away from him.

Lucius, without adjusting his line of sight, replied, 'An odd way of saying thanks.'

'What more could I possibly thank you for?'

'It appears I've raised the hackles of that waspish creature. Next to me, you'll appear the gallant hero.'

A bark of laughter escaped Alexander. 'I've no desire to be anything other than a spectator at the next bout. Perhaps you'll win that one.'

'I beg your pardon?' Lucius asked in his lazy way, which often deceived people into saying more than they ought.

Alexander naturally knew exactly what that languid tone meant and paid no heed to it when he answered, exaggerating each word as he spoke. 'Flirting? Eavesdropping? Luci, shameful.'

Lucius sniffed and raised his chin a little. 'That lady and

her sister were having a private conversation in a public space. I can hardly help that I overheard.'

'And which part of the conversation put your nose out of joint?'

'My nose is perfect, as it's always been.'

'So you quarrelled with a young lady for nothing more than sport? I wouldn't expect that of you, brother—unless, of course, she was so beautiful as to make you forget yourself. I only had sight of her back from my vantage point.' Alexander struggled but failed to hold back his grin.

The new marquess threw a sharp sidelong gaze in his brother's direction and ignored the provocation. 'That young lady is no admirer of the old marquess or the rest of the family.'

'And?' Alexander hunched a shoulder. 'She has something in common with us, if that's so.'

Lucius said nothing as he followed his brother in the direction of the farrier.

'But what you mean to say is she's no admirer of yours.' A brief, indifferent glance was all the reply Alexander received, but it was enough. 'Ha. There we have it. I'd wager she's the first woman you've met who wasn't overcome by the simple act of resting her eyes upon your person.'

Lucius smiled but rolled his eyes at his younger brother. 'Come now, Alexander, I'm not so preoccupied with my own vanity as that.'

'No, my good fellow, you are not. But it's one thing for Lady Colchester to nurse a bad opinion of you in her breast, which will no doubt already have been supplanted by a longing for your hand in that very same place, and quite another for an unknown country miss to express hers without reservation.'

'I care nothing for the good opinion of Miss Cressida Ambrose. I rather think I'll enjoy featuring as the villain of her story while in Frambury.' Lucius ignored the dubious look directed at him as they mounted their horses and turned down the lane that would lead them to Tamarix Hall.

They rode in silence, eventually coming to the ornate wrought-iron and gold gates at the beginning of the long drive to the main house. A lodgekeeper came forward, offering a wary if cordial welcome, and after a slight curve in the road, there was nothing more than a straight shot of lane and a bridge between them and the great house a quarter of a mile away, which grew steadily bigger as they approached. The golden stone reflected the sun's rays, giving the whole manor an ethereal glow.

As they came into the vast courtyard and nearer the sweeping portico, which consisted of nearly two dozen steps that looked as though they had not been scrubbed in years, and four columns the size of small giants, one with significant damage, it was Alexander who spoke first. 'Good heavens.'

'Indeed. Johnson, the steward if you recall, mentioned in one of his many letters that the estate was a bit worse for the wear.' Lucius took in the three crumbling chimneys and the half dozen or so broken windows on this side of the house.

'Did not the old marquess cut up well?'

'He died richer than Croesus, and now we see why. Come, Alexander. Let us see what joys may be found inside this pile.'

Tamarix was a vast estate. The house itself was one hundred and six rooms and unfolded this way and that. There was a maze and formal garden in the back; a kitchen garden to the side; green, undulating hills in every direction; three lakes —two small, one big; patches of forest here and there; and likely dozens of statues, temples, follies, and other smaller gardens scattered throughout the property, courtesy of the thirteen generations of Heaston men who had added, changed, or updated the property.

Lucius and Alexander were several days earlier than expected, a deliberate decision so Lucius could avoid the ceremony of being greeted by a full staff, and it was a surprised and slightly breathless stable boy who eventually came to take the reins, even as he eyed the two men with a mixture of speculation and caution.

Lucius offered the young man a kind smile. 'Lord Windmere, but you've deduced as much already, I think.'

The stable boy looked a little like a cornered cat, unsure if he should flee or fight. 'Jemmy, m'lord.'

'Helios likes you, Jemmy. Keep him in fine fettle, and we'll do quite well.'

The next surprised servant they encountered was a footman, who seemed to think Lucius's claim on the estate was a dubious one, given the mistrustful look on the lad's face, but he retrieved the butler and the housekeeper nonetheless.

'Ah, Lord Windmere, Mr Anselme, welcome to Tamarix Hall.'

Lucius fought the urge to peek at the footman.

'Thank you, Yates. Mrs Yates, I do hope you'll forgive me for bringing forward our arrival sooner than anticipated. Nothing upsets a household like early guests.'

'Not at all, my lord.' The housekeeper's response was more perfunctory than conciliatory.

'It will never do if we begin by lying to one another.' Lucius grinned, but both the butler and the housekeeper remained stiff and unsmiling. 'You both no doubt know more about me already than I will ever know about either of you, as any good servant does.' At this pronouncement, he thought he detected a slight lift of Mrs Yates's mouth. 'Therefore, it's likely you already know I am nothing like the relation from whom I inherited. It is my hope we can all rub along comfortably, seeing as we will share this house for many years.' Conscious that the footman was still hovering nearby, he suggested they repair into the small morning room just off the great entry hall.

When the door was closed, he wasted not a moment before telling the older retainers he had been made aware that the cottage to which they had removed after their wedding many years ago was inadequate for their needs and overdue for extensive repairs.

'It suits just fine, my lord,' Mrs Yates said in her stoic way.

'Perhaps it suits you, but it does not suit me to have my butler and my housekeeper living under a leaky roof with hardly two rooms between them. Tamarix provides for me, and I will provide for you. Do we understand one another?'

Mrs Yates nodded, her wide eyes the only feature betraying her surprise.

'Johnson has been overseeing the work on your new cottage and will meet with you both tomorrow to coordinate your relocation. Now, Mrs Yates, I believe a tour is in order if we are ever to find our way around without assistance.' It was a bit roughly done, but like his father, Lucius never considered himself a man to stand on ceremony with anyone, including his servants.

After a tour of the primary rooms, Mrs Yates left Alexander at the door to the room he would have while at Tamarix and sent Lucius off with detailed directions on where he could find his steward, who tended to keep to himself in a little office near the stables.

Lucius knocked on the door and waited for the steward to bid him to enter.

'Ah, Lord Windmere, I presume?' Johnson said, rising from his seat.

'Indeed. Please.' Lucius gestured to the empty seat behind the desk as he sat in one of the two chairs on the other side, silently approving the steward's placid manners—a must, he imagined, to remain employed by his grand-uncle. The man was younger than he'd expected, likely not even of an age with Lucius himself. 'At eighteen months, you've been the longest running steward here, which isn't saying much, but the offence belongs all to the previous marquess and none to you. Whether it's because you're tenacious, foolish, or both is yet to be determined.'

Lucius left a space for Johnson to respond. He'd long ago learned the power of silence.

Johnson, after half a minute or so, cleared his throat. 'If I may speak freely, sir?' Lucius inclined his head in assent. 'The previous lord, during the winter of his life, struggled not just physically due to the gout, but he laboured to recall things he said or did or dictated, and sometimes had trouble expressing himself. For the duration of my employment, he wasn't very present, so to speak.'

'I see.' It was the only time Lucius felt a twinge of compassion for his deceased relative.

His own father, at the end of his life, was often confused. Once, as he'd passed Lucius in the hall, he had shaken the book he was carrying, a finger marking a page, and said, 'I'm just off to find your mother; she'll delight in this passage.' Mrs Anselme had been gone for above a year. Another time Lucius had peered through the cracked door of his mother's sitting room and saw his father in one of the two high-backed chairs. He was drinking tea and chatting amiably with the empty space in the chair next to him, a second cup of tea on the little

34

table next to it. That time, Lucius had changed course and rather than head out for a ride, he'd gone to his room, buried his face in a pillow, and cried. He was one-and-twenty at the time.

'How is the cottage for the Yateses progressing?'

'Quite well, although the carpenter fell ill for a brief spell and some materials were delayed. That has put progress a bit behind but not so extensive as to be of concern.'

'In that same letter, you listed several other items of immediacy, but I'd like a complete list.'

'Of cottage repairs?'

'Everything. Anything that needs to be repaired, renovated, refurbished, in the main house, the grounds, tenant cottages—whatever else you can think of. We can agree the old master was a peculiar sort, one interested in his own comfort above anything else. My guess is we've got several months of work ahead of us to bring this place up to snuff, perhaps more.'

From what Lucius could tell, the only benefit to Gervais Heaston being a clutch-fist was that the coffers of Tamarix were plentiful, and he could easily afford to fix, update, and replace what was necessary, which appeared, from the short tour, to be everything.

'The lodge, some windows, and the chimneys on the east side are all in various states of disrepair, as are the carpet on the front stairs, the drapes in most of the main rooms, and several dozen chairs throughout. At least, those are the things that caught my eye when Mrs Yates took us through, although I imagine you have a much more comprehensive list—or could have quite easily. My brother will have a set of rooms here as well. You may deal with him directly, and once I've spent a little time in my own rooms, I'll produce a list of improvements for you. However, I'd prefer mine and Mr Anselme's rooms seen to after the tenant cottages.'

After further discussion about the repairs, Lucius made his exit with a tremendous sense of relief. There was quite enough to be done without needing to find a new steward.

WORD of his arrival had spread through Frambury faster than even Lucius expected, and he was inundated with callers welcoming him to the county before his valet had even unpacked his trunks.

Among the first callers was Mr Marshall Hobbs. A man, Lucius learned, in possession of a modest but comfortable home on the border of Frambury and the neighbouring village of Chilternfield, a determined wife, and a brood of very young children. Lucius typically avoided determined ladies of any variety, but Mr Hobbs, so genuine in relaying his wife's invitation to their home for an upcoming dinner party, and the accompanying note written without a hint of artifice, worked on Lucius enough, and he deigned to make Mrs Hobbs the lucky lady who would swell envy in bosoms all across the county by accepting her invitation first.

There was marked surprise on his neighbour's face when he accepted, but Lucius, for all his rakishness, devilry, and private complaints about responsibility, had had instilled in him as a boy all the morals necessary to lead a principled life, including kindness.

When he arrived at the Hobbses', he was entirely without expectations, and therefore surprised to find himself introduced to several dozen of his neighbours, including Mrs Peregrine, a widow tipping seventy whom he suspected had been a diamond in her youth. If he had hoped to see the Ambrose sisters, who were not among the guests scattered throughout the room, it was a feeling buried so deep as to be easily ignored.

'You note the mourning dress I wear.' Mrs Peregrine took in the full length of him through her quizzing glass before adding, 'You are not such a stickler as that uncle of yours, young Windmere,' addressing him in that familiar way which belonged exclusively to the elderly. 'Before you can embarrass yourself by offering condolences, let me tell you that Mr Peregrine has been gone a decade. I found that the greys and the lilacs set off the silver in my hair and simplified shopping, a necessary task that becomes increasingly difficult to abide when you get to my age.'

'I learned long ago never to come between a lady and her wardrobe.'

'Good lad. How are you enjoying this part of the country? We have very little to entertain.'

'You sell your district short, ma'am. New roads to travel, new downs to cross, new people to meet—I've been delighted at every turn.'

Mrs Peregrine gave him a look of amused disbelief that reminded him of his Aunt Bea.

'The bookshop is one of the finest I've seen in a village of any size, and I had the pleasure of meeting the Misses Ambrose while wandering among the well-stocked shelves. It's also worth mentioning that the bread from the bakery is second to none.'

Mr Hobbs, who had lingered with the pair after introductions were made, interjected then in a quiet, censorious voice. 'Those poor girls. As a father myself, it's impossible to imagine condemning my daughters as that man is doing. You don't need to look so chagrined, Mrs Peregrine. Our new lord of the manor will know soon enough what everyone else already does.'

Lucius was surprised by the disclosure and thought it rather inappropriate given the setting and his own incipient connection to these people, but he said nothing.

'Well, Mr Hobbs,' countered Mrs Peregrine, sounding a trifle vexed, 'you may as well finish what you started. No doubt you've piqued young Windmere's curiosity, although he's too well bred to say so.'

Before Lucius could move along the conversation, Mr Hobbs replied, 'There's not much more to say.'

The older lady expelled a little huff. 'There is plenty, but it can be summed up by saying Mr Ambrose cannot be bothered to chaperone his daughters himself or hire a companion to do the job. As such, they are none of them out, so to speak, although as you saw yourself, they walk into Frambury, and from time to time they visit at the rectory. No one who knows them would care if they saw fit to attend something a bit more formal. In fact we'd be very happy indeed to see them at table or dancing down the line at an assembly, but how it might look to outsiders…'

Fast was the word that came immediately to Lucius's mind. Even in the country, there would be people who would cast judgment on the sisters for not adhering to society's strictures, no matter the reason.

'Ah, Lord Windmere, are you yet acquainted with Mrs Davies? She is a friend of your cousin, Lady Lisle.'

As Lucius turned to greet the lady, he heard Mrs Peregrine say under her breath, 'Vapid woman.'

'Mrs Davies.' He extended a little bow, unwilling to exert himself to any lady claiming his cousin's friendship.

'Your dear cousin and her charming daughters are coming to stay with me for several weeks while my husband is away visiting family. I do hate being alone in that draughty old house.'

'How kind of her.'

'I'm sure she'll be pleased to see you. She has so little family left,' Mrs Davies added, with an affected sigh.

Lucius was not taken in. The woman had lost a son and husband, yes, but she also had three daughters, one of whom was married with children.

'I do believe I just saw Mr Lansdowne come in, Mrs Davies,' Mrs Peregrine said. 'You were saying recently you wanted to speak with him about a position for one of your nephews?'

When Mrs Davies was out of earshot, Lucius turned back to the old lady. 'A favourite of yours, then?'

Mrs Peregrine gave a grunting laugh. 'She's just foolish enough to think that cousin of yours a role model of some kind. She mistakes meanness for wit and cunning, gossip for conversation. A pair of tattle-mongers, the both of them.'

'How charming.'

'You have more questions, of course you do, but won't ask.' Mrs Peregrine looked at him with a twinkle in her eye. 'I, on the other hand, am too old to care. Have you spent much time in company with Lady Lisle? I imagine not, as she's never mentioned you, at least within my hearing, and she does love to chatter on about her connections.'

'Very little, ma'am, and arguably still too often.'

'The daughters?'

'A few words exchanged with the elder. She seems an unexceptional and unaffected kind of girl.'

'On that we can agree. It's a shame she was born to such a woman.'

Lucius withheld further comment, and Mrs Peregrine pressed on.

'The son?'

'Chiefly by reputation.'

'The family was given their due, but you won't find them much missed in our little part of the world. Viscount Torring wasn't a bad child, but he was overindulged, with the expected result.' She assessed his person from head to toe before adding, 'You don't look like a fool, but appearances can be deceiving and all that, so I'll say this to you, young Windmere: Lady Lisle may make some stay with Mrs Davies, but no doubt she means to wheedle an invitation from you and heaven knows what else. Her first two golden geese failed to lay eggs, but she means to make you her third.'

Her words brought forth the memory of his conversation with his Aunt Bea. He repressed a smile but reminded himself to send her an invitation to make a stay with him.

'I see.'

'I hope you do,' she replied, tapping him with the top of her walking stick. 'It's not coincidence that brings her here so soon after your arrival.'

'Should I ask how you came to these conclusions?'

Mrs Peregrine looked at him, the mischievous gleam in her eyes taking years off her countenance. 'No.'

4

*M*iles down the road, the evening unfolded at Red Fern Grange with a silent and tense dinner typical of the house. When Cressida's mother was alive, she had absorbed the brunt of her husband's displeasure with a quiet strength belied by her outward placidity. Not once did she retaliate, but she also never cowered, and she never let him break her spirit or ruin the innate kindness that defined her. Without her presence, the four Ambrose daughters worked hard to avoid their father's notice, even as they sat together around the same table.

Their father generally occupied one of two states: he was either too inebriated to get the spoon from his soup to his mouth with much success, or he wasn't drunk enough. The latter invariably led to a fist slammed on the table, a tirade about the state of the table linens or a chip in the plate (although he would never consent to replacing either), or some disparaging remark directed at Cressida, who had become his target once his wife was too sick to leave her room.

When Mr Ambrose finally rose to retire to his study to test the limits of his brandy consumption, the Ambrose daughters removed to the drawing room and sat themselves around a small fire to play vingt-un. Cressida picked at one of the many loose threads on the settee, hardly noticing anymore how run-down all the furniture in their home was.

'Maybe the new marquess has brothers, or cousins, or half-decent-looking friends,' said Rebecca, the youngest of the Ambrose girls at fourteen and an exact image of Astrid, with her dark brown hair and warm brown eyes.

'You're too young to be thinking of marriage,' replied Cora, the next in age at sixteen and an amalgamation of all her sisters—hair in between blond and brown, eyes green but not so bright or clear as Cressida's.

'And if he has brothers, out of necessity they would be younger,' chimed Cressida.

Rebecca rolled her eyes over her cards. 'Obviously, but I think we must be lucky for whatever attention we can claim. Besides, I'm not thinking of marriage for myself but for you and Astrid. Of course, I'm too young, but you two are essentially on the shelf, and if neither of you marry, what hope is there for us?'

'Becks!' It was Cora who chided her, but Cressida exchanged a glance with Astrid and the eldest cleared her throat, drawing the attention of her sisters.

'I've written to Aunt Delia.'

Cressida had been against telling the younger girls, worried about giving them false hope, but the truth was, regardless of what she and Astrid talked about and hoped for in private, if none of the sisters married soon, they would have to choose between seeking out employment that could sustain them until their father died or living with a cruel man for however many more years he thought to torment them.

'You never!'

'When? How?

'Has there been a reply?'

A cacophony of questions assaulted Astrid as she waited patiently for the two youngest to exhaust themselves.

Cora turned on Cressida. 'You're saying nothing. You knew, didn't you? Why do you two always feel it necessary to leave us out?'

'Enough, Cora.' Astrid was calm, but her tone brooked no argument. 'I had a great debate with myself as to whether I should even mention it, particularly as it has come to nothing. I sent it off many months ago, almost too long to remember.'

'What did you say? However did you even come up with the idea?'

'I've been thinking of doing so for some years, but it's never easy asking for help. Aunt Delia visited a long, long time ago, even before you were born, Rebecca, and Mama always spoke fondly of her.' She looked at her sisters, her face grim but determined. 'It's true we don't always share everything with you; we've longed to shield you from the desperation of our situation. Papa may live many more years yet, and although I cannot imagine wishing for something so terrible as his demise, the fact remains that while he's alive, we are confined to walks to the village and visits to the rectory. Father has all but cast us off, and we will inevitably fade into spinsterhood—or worse. We need someone on our side.'

Cora, who was both pragmatic and a sceptic, asked, 'How is this stranger supposed to help us?'

'Well.' Cressida drew a breath. 'We don't know exactly, as

we don't know anything of her current circumstances.' She watched her sister's mouth pull into a tight, displeased line. 'If we give our imaginations free rein, she would be able to sponsor you, Cora, in London, or Bath, or any place you might meet with eligible gentlemen.'

'Why not Astrid? Should it not be the eldest?'

Astrid, with a smile on her face that was more wistful than Cressida suspected her sister realised, replied evenly, 'Someone must remain at the Grange. If not me, then who?'

Cora suggested Cressida go with their aunt, if the possibility arose.

'No, no. I'm born to be an aunt.' Cressida meant what she said, and although she'd convinced herself of this, the truth she would not acknowledge was that it was a feeling of relatively recent development.

'What if I'd rather remain here with you all?'

'We would never force you to do anything you didn't wish.' Astrid reached for her sister's hand. 'But we want more for you, and I would encourage you to think on what you want for yourself. As it is, it's all speculation, so we need not speak on it anymore this evening.'

Rebecca, content until then as a spectator, finally spoke up. 'What if she won't help? She is *Father's* sister, is she not?'

'Mama used to say there was no love lost between our aunt and father, and rightly so. You and Cora, I suppose,' added Cressida, 'were too young to remember the few stories Mama shared.'

Delia Ambrose had been young and very much in love with the curate in her village. Her father refused to countenance what he considered a mésalliance. Her younger brother, the Ambrose girls' father, promised to take up her cause and, if needs must, help the young couple elope. Instead, he revealed her plans in exchange for a generous increase in his allowance.

Delia was confined to her room except for breakfast, dinner, and a short, carefully chaperoned constitutional, and given two options: exile to America to stay with a relation she'd never met, because her father would harbour no traitor to the family name under his roof, or marriage to the only son of a couple who lived in the next county. Delia married just weeks later.

Rebecca asked, 'What if they have their own brood of children—a gaggle of single daughters—and Aunt Delia's husband has no interest in taking on another?'

'Those are very sensible questions and very real possibilities.' Astrid answered with the ease and tranquillity of someone who had already thought through such possibilities. 'If that's so, we are no worse off than we are now.'

Cora sighed. 'All those ifs. I feel rather hopeless.'

'Well,' said Cressida, in her resolute way, 'we are all together in hope and in hopelessness.'

In hers and Astrid's room that night, Cressida found herself thinking of her mother—thinking how easy it was for a woman to marry a man without knowing anything of substance about him.

As a child, she'd often felt confused and angry with her mother because she couldn't understand why her mama never told her father to stop—to stop yelling, to stop throwing things, to stop rattling the house with his anger. When Cressida tried to intervene, he dealt with her the same, with a backhand to her cheek, with her body tossed into a wall—no matter that she was six, or ten, or fourteen.

As an adult, Cressida understood that there no recourse for a married woman, particularly one with children and without other family. She understood that taking what-ever he wanted to give was easier, safer, than taking what he would give if he was challenged. The only benefit to their mother falling ill, if there was one, was that even their father wouldn't hit a woman on her deathbed. It never mattered which course Cressida's thoughts took, they always ended in the same place: agonising, rooted pain for her mama, what she'd endured, what she'd deserved and never had.

'Cressie?'

Cressida was startled by her sister's voice. She'd thought Astrid had drifted to sleep by her rhythmic breathing. 'Yes?'

'You have made clear your desire to be an aunt—'

'The kind who gives her sisters' children too many sweets than are good for them and who helps her dearest sister manage her largesse.' Cressida knew the direction of her sister's thoughts and was desperate to dodge the impending conversation, as she had in the past. Except here, in their room, there was no escape.

'Yes, but even if our aunt agrees to host Cora, I worry she is still full young to be married.'

'I know you think it should be one of us—me, really, since you prefer to keep an eye on the Grange, and I don't fault you for that—but I could never abide giving control to another man, not when we've yet to even relinquish the hold Father has over us.'

'Not all men are bad, dear one.'

'No, but I've no faith in myself to know the difference.'

'You're too hard on yourself. More to the point, there's so much uncertainty—'

'There's so much uncertainty in marriage. We, in our current circumstances, at least have some idea of what may come. In marriage, who is ever certain until it is too late?'

A fraught silence pulled at the space between the sisters. Astrid was the first to speak. 'Mrs Peregrine mentioned to me recently that Mr St John would like to find a wife, someone to keep house, to look after his children.'

'Astrid?' Cressida's heart thumped in her chest.

'He's kind. It would be a good match for me.'

Cressida sat forward with a jolt. 'You can't mean it. He's old! He can hire a governess if he needs someone to watch his children.'

'He's thirty-seven or thirty-eight and not unattractive,' retorted Astrid, expelling an impatient sigh.

'And he will do what? Storm the gate in front of the house, demand Father release us to his care, and we all remove to St John Lodge? That poor man, with all his affability, can hardly manage his servants, much less that beast in the study. Besides, with his two children and a spinster sister already under his roof, he can hardly afford a wife and her three single sisters.'

Astrid had risen also, and although the curtains were closed over the moonlight night, their eyes had adjusted enough to see the shape of one another. 'You may come off your high horse. It's not as though he's made me an offer. In fact, I think it unlikely given how little we see of him, of anybody.'

'But if he made an offer, you would accept it? That's what you're saying?'

'What I am saying is, if by chance he made me an offer, I would consider it.' After a long moment, she added in a quiet voice, 'And very likely accept.'

Cressida tossed the bedclothes aside and began to pace the length of the smallish room the two sisters shared, unable to remain seated when so much nervous energy coursed through her. 'Everything you've said about wanting to remain at Red Fern, was that all lies?'

'No. But removing to a house in the same district as the Grange is not the same as being away in Bath for half the year.'

'Fine, but what of your happiness, Astrid? Don't you ever want to know what that feels like? True happiness? Contentment?' Cressida hadn't realised tears had formed in her eyes until she was brushing them from her cheek.

Astrid climbed from the bed and stepped in front of her sister, bracing a hand on each of her shoulders. 'How can we even know what that is? What I do know is nothing could make me happier than being able to help my sisters. That is enough for me.'

Cressida was near enough to her sister to make out the earnest expression on her face. She didn't know what to say, so instead of saying anything she leaned in and placed a light kiss on her cheek before retreating to her side of the bed.

This time, Cressida was certain Astrid had fallen asleep. Her sister was snoring softly, a sound Cressida found calming. She had long admired her sister's ability to fall quickly into sleep, into dreams.

Dreams were something Cressida had abandoned piece by piece as the years ticked by. The dream her mother would recover. The dream her father would one day wake up and decide he'd raged enough. The dream her father wouldn't wake up at all. The dream of loving and being loved.

The last one, a dream she seemed to have been born into the world with and had clung to in those long nights she'd lain awake with a poultice on her cheek, was the hardest to let go. That, at least, had felt like something over which she had some little control—the ability to say 'yes' or 'no' to a man. But her mother, before her death, had told Cressida something that made even that dream feel impossible. It was a secret Mrs Ambrose had kept to protect her daughter. It explained why his anger had only two targets, and it meant that Cressida, should she ever fall in love, would either enter into marriage with a secret from her husband or risk being cast off by the man to whom she gave her heart.

5

---

*T*here was nothing Lucius expected more than the visit Lady Lisle paid him at Tamarix, accompanied by her two daughters, the day after her arrival. He kept them waiting for above half an hour and entered the small green salon with the imperturbable and aloof countenance of one assured of his own authority.

'Lady Lisle, Miss Heaston, Miss…'

'Cassandra, my lord, my youngest.'

He offered a perfunctory bow and did not ring for refreshment as he took a seat in a chair removed a little distance from the ladies.

Lady Lisle, in a hat with too large a plume and a morning dress adorned with too much lace, watched him with critical eyes. 'You'll forgive my paying the visit—there can be no care for propriety where family is concerned.'

Lucius made no reply. The woman in front of him had known, at least since her son died, if not long before, who the next heir was and had taken that entire length of time to conclude she ought to pursue the connection. Her husband had carried on the family feud of his father and his father's father, and Lucius would give her credit for her familial loyalty. Had she made some attempt at reconciliation in the months after Lord Lisle's death, Lucius might have received her, if not with warmth, at least with indifference. Unfortunately, there were several kinds of people whom he could not abide: liars, cheats, and sycophants were at the top of the list. There were no illusions where he was concerned. He doubted not that she struggled between a desire to malign him and a desire to shackle one of her daughters to him, but that she wanted him for a son-in-law was certain, and she would do whatever lay in her power to see that plan to fruition.

'A capricious thing, family. Do you not agree?'

Her ladyship offered what he supposed was a smile. 'It's not for me to judge the capricious nature of anything. I changed my own hat three times before leaving Mrs Davies's home this morning.'

Once again, he remained silent, enjoying Lady Lisle's visible struggle to maintain her composure in the face of such inhospitality. He noted, with a quick glance at the daughters, who remained silent, that the elder looked resigned to the situation and the younger uncomfortable.

The woman across from him raised her chin a little so that she peered down the length of her own nose as she spoke. 'It must be a great change for you, retiring to the country for a time, when you're so well known for your enjoyment of town. For my part, I've always considered this place the most charming locality, and nothing restores one quite like gusts of bracing country air.'

Lucius repressed a smirk and pulled out his pocket watch to check the time before issuing a reply. Her false friendship had lasted approximately four minutes. If he were less a gentleman, he would ask her outright in the presence of her daughters if their happiness was of so little value that she was willing to overlook his *enjoyment* of town just to keep herself tied to the title.

'It is true, ma'am, there are a great many entertainments to be had in town—and of greater variety than the country—but I'm a man who gives duty as much weight as pleasure.'

A faint flush spread across Lady Lisle's face, but she bravely launched another attack.

'How admirable. This duty must seem more of a burden to a man who wasn't raised to such an august position. Your mother came from trade, unless I am much mistaken?'

An odd tactic, he mused, for a woman hoping to bind him to her family. Then again, she was faced with the man who, to her, must seem the thief in possession of what should have belonged to her husband and son.

'You are thinking of my grandmama, whose father came from a long line of lacemakers and whose family owned the largest manufactory in France, in addition to several others further abroad. My father relocated production to English soil to minimise travel. Those centres, upon my parents' deaths, became mine. No doubt your own closet holds some Anselme lace.'

'Oh, I should very much doubt it.' Lady Lisle rushed through a reply as Lucius examined the lace trimming on her dress, the fichu tucked in the top, the delicate shawl wrapped about her shoulders.

'That,' he said, his eyes on the space between her throat and her chest, 'is embroidered cotton, of course, but the trim of your dress is a blond bobbin lace, and your shawl is Cecily from Bedfordshire. That pattern was my grandmother's favourite, and very aptly named for her.'

Lady Lisle's eyes went wide as she fingered the lace draped around her shoulders, and he wondered if she'd go home and consign her clothing to the fire.

'I could tell you which shop sold it to you, which linen-draper supplied the fabric for your dress, and where in Cheap-side you could get that same blond lace for less, not that I would ever presume you shop in such an area as that' The woman's mouth had dropped open a little in surprise, and Lucius took the opportunity presented by her silence to rise, signalling the end of the painful meeting and effectively thwarting any response.

'May you have a pleasant stay with Mrs. Davies, madam. Ladies.'

He opened the door himself and let the footman see the party out while he went in search of his brother. He found Alexander in the billiard room lining up a shot. The younger Anselme didn't remove his eyes from the cue ball as he asked, 'What think you of your intended?'

Rather than dignify that question with a response, Lucius simply walked behind his brother and bumped the cue stick, making Alexander miss his shot.

'A real beauty, then.' Alexander laughed, not at all put off by his older brother's antics.

'You've seen both the daughters in town, have you not?'

'Have I? When?' The question was asked with genuine curiosity.

'However should I know?'

'You said it.'

'Insomuch that *I've* seen them, and as you attend the same functions as I do, it seems a reasonable assumption to make that *you've* seen them as well.'

'Yes, well, their mama I remember with clarity.' Alexander

walked round the table to take another shot. 'Your indifference rather enrages her, I think.'

Lucius tipped his head in agreement. 'Yet I am the matrimonial target for one of her daughters.'

'Naturally.'

Lucius scoffed. 'There's nothing natural about pawning a daughter off on a man who will never care for her, for the sake of pin money and a title.'

Alexander knocked a ball into the corner pocket, walked to the wall to retrieve another cue, and handed it to his brother. 'Never say never, Luci.' It was something Alexander said often enough, and Lucius never lost the desire to shake his brother each time. Their views of marriage, of romantic feelings and relationships, would never align, and Lucius hadn't the slightest idea how to explain his reasoning in a way that wouldn't give pain to his dear younger brother.

The thing of it was, it had taken four long years for their mama to pass on from this world. While Alexander was away at school, Lucius had remained at home to care for her. What he went through in those years he would never forget, and the resolution he made he would never absolve.

Her illness started slowly—a muscle twitch here, a slurred word there. Eventually weight loss, tremors, and fatigue followed. As her condition worsened, Lucius's father withdrew into himself, unable to watch the thing he loved most in the world slip away a little more each day. A nursemaid was brought in to help with her personal needs, but it was Lucius who came down from Cambridge and stepped up in all other ways. He spoon-fed her at each meal, read to her in the evenings, and pushed her around the garden in a bath-chair when the weather permitted. He often brushed her hair, rubbed her favourite cream into her hands, and wrapped her in his arms whenever the shaking was more than she could bear.

Alexander would visit from Eton for Christmas and Twelfth Night and at the end of every term. He could see with his own eyes that their mama was not well, but he always went back to school, back to the life he should be living as a boy—the life Lucius wanted at least one of them to have. It meant, however, that Alexander never understood the extent of their mother's illness, never understood the sacrifices Lucius made, or the crack of pain that started small and grew to a great yawning pit within him.

One day, while he read to his mama from her favourite book in front of a cosy fire in the library, the rise and fall of her chest slowed then stopped; the faint hold her hand had on his went slack, and Lucius knew his mother's spirit had left her body. He should have rung the bell, called for his father, but instead, he clutched his mother's hand to his chest and sobbed. She was the best of everything rolled into a single person.

After her death, Lucius's papa, once a strong, vibrant, and capable man, became a shell of himself, forcing Lucius, at just twenty, to raise his brother, to take the reins of the estate, to oversee a veritable business empire, with very little functional knowledge of how to do any of it. Lucius had had a deep sense of responsibility ingrained in him from an early age, knowing as he did that one day he would take over Branford Park, but he resented the early arrival of those responsibilities. He resented being unable to do what other young men his age were doing, but with a brother too young to be independent and a father too eaten up by grief to leave his bed, he'd had very little choice in the matter. It wasn't many years on before his father followed his mother to the grave, and the idea that there might be any kind of reprieve was entirely banished.

In those years, there were many nights Lucius had lain awake wondering which was worse: watching his mother fade from illness or his father fade from sadness. There were nights that he indulged in fits of pity and melancholy. There were nights he wondered what it would be like to love a woman so much that when she left the earth, she would take his spirit with her, if not his body too. Then there were the nights he would think of his invalid mother, of his useless father, of every obligation that awaited him once he rose from the bed, and he would imagine the day he could do as he pleased. Lucius loved his family, but he resented the way his life had unfolded, and he decided, when all was still and silent, and not even the bright white light of the moon cut through the heavy velvet drapes, he had no room in his life for anything or anyone else.

he warmth of the sun, the sting of the crisp spring air when it breezed across Cressida's cheeks and her bare arms, was almost enough to restore her spirits and clear away the thoughts that weighed heavily upon her mind.

'Well, now,' Astrid remarked with a contented sigh as she sank onto the blankets spread atop Dryce Hill, where the Ambrose girls and Sophia had ventured for a picnic. 'If there's a more peaceful way to waste away a day, I cannot think of it.'

Cressida offered a wan smile as she looked out over the downs unfolding before them. 'Sophia, tell us, have you met with those guests of the Hobbses' yet?'

'Unfortunately,' Sophia began, pausing to take a small bite of cake, 'their plans have been delayed, and they are not likely to be looked for for some weeks yet.'

'That's too bad.'

'Yes, but I did discover who they're expecting—two gentlemen and a lady. Relatives of Mrs Hobbs, I believe, although to what degree I'm still unaware.'

Cressida finally pulled her eyes from the landscape in front of her to arch her brows at her friend. 'So, not a complete waste of an evening.'

Sophia smiled down at the piece of bread in her hand, a tell-tale sign she was hoarding information. 'Hardly that. The news of the delay is certainly disappointing, but the discovery of the persons coming to our little piece of country rewarding.' All the Ambrose sisters knew her well enough to catch their breath in anticipation. Sophia was their primary source of town news—nearly their only source—and she never disappointed. 'Even more rewarding, however, was making the acquaintance of the new marquess myself.'

Excited gasps burst from the younger Ambrose sisters, the eldest smiled, and Cressida went so far as to raise her brows in surprise and curiosity.

Rebecca, with all the impatience customary of youth, demanded, 'Well?'

'I was quite right,' replied Sophia. 'He's charming—'

'But is he handsome? That's all that can matter,' Rebecca interrupted.

'Goodness, Becks,' chided Cora. 'Sometimes I wonder if we got all the sense and left none for you.'

Rebecca shrugged her sister's teasing words off, saying, 'He's so far above our touch. All we can hope from the acquaintance is the pleasure of a fine countenance to admire. Who's sensible now?'

Sophia interjected before the teasing could turn into something more, as it sometimes did between the younger sisters. 'I've not much to compare him with, but I daresay he's the most handsome man I've seen. How you were able to string together two words,' Sophia said, turning her attention to

Cressida, 'much less give him a set-down, is well beyond my comprehension. I don't think my breath steadied for a full minute after Mr Hobbs introduced him to our party.'

'A set-down!' exclaimed Cora.

Cressida tossed Sophia an ungrateful glance. 'It seems our friend must have indulged in one too many glasses of wine. Lord Windmere is an odious, unfeeling sort of man.'

Sophia reached for a piece of cheese, unperturbed by her friend's contradictory statement. 'Your sister's prejudices obscure her judgement. Although'—she pursed her lips before continuing—'I will own there are some here who cling to their scepticism.'

'Why?'

Rebecca's innocent question sent cautious looks rippling around the group of ladies—Sophia to Cressida, Cressida to Astrid. Astrid gave an insignificant shrug, and Cora watched all of them with round, curious eyes.

Cressida finally answered. 'He's a rakehell.'

'What's that to do with anything?' questioned Rebecca.

Sophia clapped her hands in delight. 'Exactly my stance, you dear girl.'

Cressida looked heavenward and shook her head. 'Perhaps fathers, mothers, and shopkeepers worry about their daughters. Perhaps tenants worry about the marquess's ability to manage his property if he's more interested in—' She came to an abrupt halt and pinched her lips together.

'In what?' asked Astrid, with a wide, knowing smile.

Cressida cleared her throat. 'Erm, pursuits. Feminine pursuits.'

Rebecca, looking a little bewildered, asked, 'Lord Windmere trims bonnets and paints in watercolour?'

'No. Those aren't—that's not quite what I mean.' Cressida paused, realising the mistake she'd made and the tough position in which she'd placed herself. 'Not that kind of, erm, feminine pursuits. Rather,' she delicately cleared her throat, 'pursing females.'

No less confused, Rebecca pushed on. 'But who could he possibly pursue here? The Cadens are both betrothed, Miss Samon and her sisters all have horse faces, and wouldn't a marquess marry some heiress, or lady, or both?'

Cora looked as if she might take offence at her sister's guileless statement, but the elder three girls offered indulgent smiles even as Cressida responded with a gentle reprimand. 'Just so, sweetling, but we need to work a bit more on your conduct.' What she really meant was that she and Astrid needed to take the youngest a bit more in hand. Rebecca was in the awkward space between being a girl and becoming a young lady, and with so much uncertainty ahead, the two eldest had not been as disciplined with the youngest as they could have been.

'If there is any truth in what's printed in the papers,' added Sophia, 'Rebecca is quite correct. Aside from Mrs Peregrine and several other matrons, we've no widows within several miles, and certainly no ladies to draw the notice of a man like him. All that aside, the Heastons were never friendless when they lived here, even if they were not so well liked by those of us with good sense. There are still those like Mrs Davies or Mr Grant from Chilternfield who will take Lord Windmere in dislike on principle.'

'Who is Mr Grant?' asked Cora.

'A friend of Viscount Torring,' replied Astrid, sparing Cressida the need to say that man's name. 'Sophia, are you quite all right?'

The rector's daughter had buried her head in her hands and her shoulders were shaking as if she might be crying. When she raised her head, her eyes were indeed brimming, with tears of amusement. 'It's only that I cannot stop picturing the most *awful* thing—Lord Windmere and Mrs Peregrine. Could you imagine?' Saying so aloud rent a peal of laughter from every young lady in the cosy group.

The joyful sound was carried off in the wind as Cora and Rebecca settled into discussing a book they'd been reading to one another before bed, Astrid and Sophia began a game of cribbage, and Cressida reclined on her forearms, her face tilted to the sky, eyes closed. She felt herself drifting but hadn't realised how close to sleep she'd been until the shock of a small hand closing around her forearm and the gasp accompanying it jolted her awake. Before she could ask Sophia what was the matter, the latter said in a quiet voice trembling with excitement. 'Lord Windmere.'

All the Ambrose sisters followed Sophia's line of sight, a little way down the grassy knoll on which they were seated. There, at the bottom, was the man from the bookshop, perched astride a great beast of a horse and accompanied by another gentleman of similar colouring and form. Cressida rose to a sitting position to better watch their progress and fought to keep her expression neutral as both turned and encouraged their mounts up the hill.

'Miss Harland, how do you do? No, please, do remain seated. You are all so charmingly grouped. Allow me to introduce my brother, Mr Anselme, who was sadly absent when I had the pleasure of making your acquaintance at the Hobbses'.'

Cressida thought his eyes flicked her direction as he dismounted, but it was so fleeting that perhaps she only imagined it. She folded her hands in her lap and realised her palms were hot and a little damp.

'If I may,' Sophia replied from her seat on the blanket, introducing each Ambrose sister and inviting the gentlemen to join their little party to the delight of some and the chagrin of one.

Cressida, who levelled a hard stare at Lord Windmere, missed the apprehensive look on her eldest sister's face and the speculative one on Mr Anselme's.

'We'd be delighted, wouldn't we, Alexander?' The new marquess didn't wait for his brother to respond before seating himself near Cressida—not that she thought anyone's opinion mattered to the man besides his own.

She turned so that her next words might only be heard by him. 'Would you not prefer to stand some little way off? One cannot both partake in a conversation and eavesdrop upon it at the same time, and I know how fond you are of the latter.'

Lord Windmere offered her a lazy half smile at odds with the sharp glint in his eyes. Cressida studied their colour, the dark blue outline of his irises at contrast with the unique shade it edged. As the sun caught his face just right, she saw a small ring of gold hugging his pupil, and a few tiny flecks of light brown peppered throughout.

He quietly cleared his throat, and Cressida sucked in a sharp breath as she became aware just how long she'd been staring at him. When he eventually responded to her jibe, his voice was little more than a whisper, but his words rose and fell and coursed within her all the same. 'If my person is to occupy a share of your conversation—and your thoughts—I'd just as soon have my say this time around.'

Heat crept up her neck, and she turned her attention to the blades of grass she was pulling through her fingers. 'You are quite right, my lord,' she said, thinking of Astrid's earlier words. 'We should not have been speaking so in public.' When he made no reply, she prompted, 'Now that I've made my apology, you may make yours.'

'Was that an apology? I must not have been giving your words the full attention they no doubt deserved. Miss Ambrose,' he said, turning his attention to Astrid and leaving Cressida no opportunity for a rebuttal, 'I've been told that one day you will be at the helm of Red Fern Grange.'

Astrid's eyes went wide only for a moment before she schooled her features. 'Yes, that's right.'

Cressida looked at the man sitting near her, expecting to see mockery or laughter writ in his features, but his smile was all warmth and genuine friendliness, and she felt a prick of something within that she could not identify, except to say it made her feel a little unsteady.

'I've a little experience with such matters,' he said. 'No doubt you've learned more than enough to do your family credit, but should you have any interest in discussing irrigation techniques or four-field crop rotation, I'm always willing to impart what I've learned and to learn from others.'

Astrid expressed her interest and appreciation and thanked him for the kind offer. Too kind, Cressida thought, and she wondered what he was hoping to gain from such a thing. She wouldn't ask, but even if she wanted to, it was Rebecca who spoke up next.

'Lord Windmere, what exactly does a marquess do?'

'Well,' he began, turning a little in Rebecca's direction and giving Cressida an unobstructed view of his perfect profile. 'That depends on the marquess. Historically, he was relied on to defend land against hostile neighbours; the word itself derives from marches. These days, however, a marquess's primary responsibility is to the people on his land—tenants, farmers, neighbours—and of course sitting in the House of Lords.'

'Yes,' Rebecca replied with some impatience, 'but can you do all that if you're preoccupied with pursuing females?' Her question, asked with genuine wide-eyed curiosity, silenced the general buzz of chatter among the group, and Cressida, who'd just popped a chunk of cheese into her mouth, coughed as she struggled to swallow it.

Without so much as looking at her, Lord Windmere brought a large hand to her back and gave it a few firm pats. On the last, his hand lingered only as long as it took for one second to tick to the next. The gesture was familiar, but the touch—his touch—felt intimate. Despite the warmth of the sun upon her, under the muslin of her dress, Cressida's skin prickled. She looked askance at him, but his attention was still on the youngest Ambrose.

'Your thoughtful concern does you credit, Miss Rebecca. Let me reassure you, my responsibilities as marquess will in no way be hindered by, as you phrased it, pursuing females.' His reply was serious, but Cressida was close enough to him to notice the little twitch pulling the corner of his lips.

She fought back her own smile in response, but the desire to do so disappeared entirely when Rebecca looked directly at her and said, 'See, you may tell me I'm right.'

There was no chance of Cressida doing any such thing, but before she could offer up another topic for discussion, Lord Windmere, once more with that devilish and teasing smirk on his face, asked Rebecca what she was right about.

'About there being no females in our little slice of the country worthy your notice.'

Mr Anselme laughed outright at this absurd pronouncement; Sophia and Cora hid their amusement behind a hand; Astrid scolded Rebecca for her total want of conduct; and Lord Windmere himself chuckled, but Cressida could only wonder why it should irritate her that the new marquess found anything amusing in such a statement.

7

*D*espite the multitude of invitations stacking up on Lucius's desk, he declined them all in favour of investing his time in Tamarix. He was certain every family within a ten-mile radius must know he'd arrived, that he had been seen in company with his neighbours and, he thought grimly as he opened and discarded one invitation after the other, that he was without a wife.

In London, his rakehell reputation had spared him from all but the most determined matchmaking mamas—those with a gaggle of daughters or husbands in need of a great wave of cash—and he wore it like armour. He sighed. Even his reputation wouldn't be enough now that he was titled, and in the meanwhile, country matrons were another animal entirely, faced with fewer prospects for their progeny in their small villages.

That little matter—his being a bachelor—was a complication he'd managed to ignore for the last few years. But now that he was in fact the marquess, he thought of little else except what would happen if he tripped down the stairs and broke his neck, if he choked on his soup, if he managed to drown in the lake round the back of the house.

He imagined Alexander forced into a role he didn't want, much as Lucius had been all those years ago. He imagined his affable and kind younger brother finding himself caught in a trap before he even realised one had been set. He imagined Alexander stumbling through a speech before Parliament or trying to make head or tail of the bills he would vote on. Alexander was many things, but he had never been comfortable on display. It was during moments like these Lucius wondered if everything he had done in service to his brother had reaped more harm than good.

'What are the odds, do you suppose, of a family having four children all blessed with good looks?'

Lucius looked up from the stack of papers scattered in front of him and watched his brother take up a seat in the high-backed leather chair across from the desk.

'Well?'

He winged an eyebrow in surprise. 'I did not realise you required an answer.' Nor did he realise the Ambrose sisters had taken up residence in his brother's mind even a sennight after their encounter with them. He pushed a pair of star-tlingly light green eyes from his mind. 'There are any number of families I could name with brothers and sisters who all can claim an equal share of fine features.'

'But the Ambrose sisters—I speak mostly of the elder, but the younger two deserve honourable mentions and will garner their fair share of praise in a few years more. Miss Harland, too, is quite an attractive lady. That this little slice of the country could harbour such treasures—'

Lucius interjected before his brother lost himself to rhapsodising. 'Yes, it's always shocking to discover beauty exists outside of town, is it not?' His tone was dry, mordant.

'Thou doth protest too much.'

'That's not—No matter.' He shook his head and returned to the page in his hand, a note from Mr Harland informing him of a forthcoming afternoon of tea and cards at the rectory, to which both Anselme gentlemen were invited. He heard the leather groan as Alexander shifted in the seat.

'I see why you chose to factor as the villain in Miss Cressida's story.'

Lucius remembered saying as much but failed to catch his brother's meaning and against his own good sense turned a questioning look in his direction.

Alexander smiled in return. The kind of triumphant smile that reminded Lucius of when he used to let Alexander win at cricket or cards or any other game they played. 'It's quite simple. If you're the villain, you cannot also be the hero.'

'For goodness' sake, Alex,' Lucius scoffed.

'Thou doth continue to protest.'

'You know better than anyone that I do not trifle with innocents.'

'Yes. Exactly my point.'

'Do you feel you're being clever?'

'Hardly, but you're being obtuse. I'd never accuse you of *trifling* with a young lady of gentle breeding. Rather I'm suggesting you find yourself *attracted* to one.'

Lucius was out of patience and felt his restraint couldn't be far behind. No one knew how to wheedle him like his brother. 'I've agreed with you that they are pretty girls. Now, if that's all.' He made a vague gesture to his desk.

'You haven't, at least not until just then, but that is not the point I'm making.'

'Ah. I wasn't sure you had one to make. Perhaps you can come to it then.'

Alexander shook his head and looked heavenward, as if he was the one exercising inhuman levels of tolerance during this conversation. 'Should we call Cook for some tea and cakes, Luci? You seem a bit out of sorts.'

'I'm not a child, Alex,' Lucius bit back, rising from his chair with a mind to physically remove his brother from the study.

'And yet…' Alexander laughed openly when Lucius glared at him and carried on, even as a storm brewed on his brother's face. 'Only you know your reasons, real or imagined, for going about in the manner you choose. I'm simply suggesting you ask yourself this question: what would happen if you didn't act the rake, the villain? I'll say no more.' And he didn't. The younger Anselme rose from the chair and left the study without another word.

Lucius watched him go; the only sign his brother's words had had any impact was the clenching of his jaw and the twitch of that muscle beneath the taut skin of his cheek. He pulled the bell and sat back down as he waited for Mrs Yates to answer his summons.

'You rang for me, m'lord?'

'Yes, Mrs Yates, do come in. This morning Johnson informed me another fortnight should see the work complete on your new cottage.'

'That's mighty quick work, sir.'

'Yes, well,' Lucius had no interest in admitting he'd asked Johnson to give the project priority, so he changed the subject. 'Has the doctor seen little Martin Sheffield?'

Lucius thought he detected some softening of Mrs Yates' features at the mention of that rambunctious cub.

'Yesterday, sir. He set the arm, and although it is now in a sling, the doctor suggested Martin remain abed for a little longer if he wants to avoid reinjuring it.'

'That's a tall order for a boy of seven,' he replied. 'I'll take a basket tomorrow, if you can have one prepared, and see if I can't bribe him into being a good lad. How are we coming with shoes for the Warren clan? Nine children. Can you imagine?'

Lucius had begun once more to sift through the invitations on his desk but looked up when Mrs Yates' voice failed to fill the silence following his question. She was looking at him, but her eyes were apprehensive, and she was worrying her hands.

'Mrs Yates?'

'I spoke with Mr Harland. The church has received a great many donations but only two pairs of shoes in the correct sizes. There are funds, but...' She trailed off and looked at the floor.

It took Lucius a moment to understand what the older woman was saying. 'Let me guess. The Warrens aren't keen to accept a financial handout, although they are certainly entitled to one.'

'Just so, sir. Mr Warren works hard, but as you said, nine children. It's a point of pride for them both, I daresay.'

He sat back and turned his gaze towards the ceiling, as he often did when sorting through a problem. He suspected the old marquess, if he'd even been aware of such a need among those in the parish, would have thought it the Warrens' just deserts for having more children than they could afford. He unlocked a drawer and counted out a small stack of bills, holding it out to his shocked housekeeper.

'Have a new pair made for each child. The elder I suspect are nearly done growing, but the younger will certainly need another pair before winter. May I depend on you to take notice and come to me should such a need arise?'

Mrs Yates looked between the funds in her hand and her employer. 'Certainly, my lord.'

'Good. That will be all.'

She nodded and made to leave.

'Oh, and Mrs Yates?'

She turned, still wearing a look of amazement. 'Sir?'

'I'd prefer if you could contrive to have the shoes delivered without assigning me any of the credit.'

A mix of puzzlement and curiosity flitted over her features, but she agreed without asking questions. He felt only a small degree of guilt for giving her such a task, but if she was to remain in his employ it was best she accustomed herself to such challenges. His father had raised him to believe the act of charity was always better performed without recognition for it. That, and Lucius despised being the recipient of people's gratitude. He hated being thanked for doing what he easily could and should, and he couldn't abide the idea of people feeling obligated to him, particularly those in contrasting circumstances to his own.

After dismissing Mrs Yates, he rose, poured himself two fingers of brandy, and returned to his seat to read his Aunt Margot's letter. It was lucky for him all her daughters were married off and her eldest son the recipient of a tidy inheritance himself. She had, however, a younger son very soon completing his Grand Tour and wondered if perhaps there was some little thing Lucius could do for his cousin. He would, of course. He always did.

He sighed and gazed out over his new property. The fields were in surprisingly good shape —much better than any of the structures. From the day of his arrival, he had been working hard and fast to tick the boxes of the ever-growing to-do list Johnson had compiled. Despite hiring extra labourers, he suspected he'd be at Tamarix another two months, at which point he'd have just enough time to return to London for the close of the season, or perhaps go directly on to Brighton.

Regardless of how long he stayed, or where he went after, whether to London or Brighton or the moon, he was only delaying the inevitable. He would do what he'd always done: his duty, even if that meant consigning himself to a life he didn't want to save his brother from the same fate. He'd done so before; he could do so again.

8

'Perhaps I should have taken orders,' Alexander commented as he and Lucius turned their horses down the drive towards the Harland home.

'Mr Harland is blessed with good fortune.' Lucius took in the charming brick façade of the home, the leafy green vines climbing up its side, the stark white sash of the windows, and guessed the building to be greater in size than Red Fern Grange, which they had ridden past that day they came across the ladies on Dryce Hill. He had been shocked by the conditions of that house and its surrounding fields from just the little he could see from the road.

Alexander, eyes still on the house, replied, 'I own to having been curious as to how tea and a small card party could be comfortably had in a rectory, but this is hardly the cosy cottage of my imagination.'

A boy came to take their horses, and when they were announced to the general company already gathered in a large sunny parlour, the lady of the house received them with an unaffected smile and warm welcome.

'We're so pleased to count two more young people among our numbers.'

'You flatter me, Mrs Harland, by counting me as a young person.'

She waved off Lucius's words with a dainty flick of her wrist. 'Nonsense. You young people always think you're older than you are—you can't even begin to comprehend the meaning of the word until you have children who steal the colour from your hair, the bloom from your cheeks, and all your peace. Now, make yourselves comfortable. We don't stand on ceremony at these little parties,' she said, shooing them further inside the room and intercepting her husband, who had approached with claims that young people had much better ways to spend their time than engaged in dull pleasantries with their host and hostess.

Lucius, who had the keen sensation he was being watched, a feeling he was all too familiar with, ticked his eyes right and left, noting a few familiar faces, a few new ones, and, to his great surprise, several of the Ambrose sisters. His eyes alighted on Miss Cressida just as her own gaze darted in another direction. He held back a smile and ignored the strange urge to saunter over to where she was. Instead, he accepted Miss Harland's offer of tea and followed her to the tea things, which brought him nearer Miss Cressida's more remote corner of the room.

'That's it for me,' exclaimed the young man who sat across from her. 'I'll need time to recover before a rematch. Is forever too long, do you think?'

The laugh on her lips died away as Lucius came nearer.

'Lord Windmere, this is my youngest brother, Mr George Harland,' Miss Harland said as she handed him his cup.

'A pleasure.'

'Not when one is getting trounced! I wish you great good luck,' he said, gesturing to his now-vacant seat.

Lucius looked at Cressida. She had come to stand, and her eyes were hard with displeasure. He smiled and sat down, all but forcing her to do the same. 'What are we playing? Best of three? Of five?' He held out the deck of cards for her, nearly dropping them when her bare fingertips grazed over his upturned palm.

'How many will it take for you to accept defeat?' she asked as she shuffled. 'I'd tell you it's rude to stare, but I suspect you already know and do not care.'

Lucius *was* staring. He felt both as if he'd never really seen her before and as though every feature was familiar and dear to him. 'I must beg your pardon. I had not realised cribbage was such a competitive sport, and I was making a silent vow to give you, and the game, my full attention.'

'I'd expect something more original from a hardened flirt.'

The comment niggled him, and he responded with more asperity than intended. 'Is that your own assessment or one from the papers?'

'Does it matter? Would one or the other make it any less true?' Her eyes held his in challenge.

'Do you enjoy being contrary? I pity the man who takes you for a wife.'

Her eyes narrowed. 'You may save it. I've no plans to take a husband.'

Lucius lifted a brow in a studied show of disbelief. 'You would prefer what—schoolteacher? Governess? I doubt companion would suit.'

'I'll remain at the Grange and help Astrid manage it, when the time comes,' she said, looking down at her lap and smoothing out her skirt.

The movement drew his attention, and he noticed for the first time how faded the material of her dress was, the little signs of wear that couldn't be hidden by clever stitching. A burst of anger at her irresponsible father coursed through him, and he snuffed it out as quickly as it came.

'Until then?' Asking was bad *ton*, but he didn't feel the least bit guilty for putting the blame for his bad manners on her impertinence. She shifted a little in the chair and pinched her lips together, as if she wasn't sure how to respond to such a direct question. Her hesitation surprised him.

When she finally spoke, it wasn't to deliver an answer but an insult, with an unflinching and unapologetic glare. 'I pity the woman who takes you and your insufferable lack of manners for a husband.'

He chuckled. 'Come now, you've seen my name bandied about in the papers enough to know how unlikely it is that such an event will come to pass, have you not?'

Was that a hint of pink suffusing her cheeks? Lucius hoped so.

'It's your "go", sir.'

He looked down at the cards on the table, which he didn't remember playing. 'So it is.' He pegged his point on the cribbage board and counted first, as Miss Cressida had dealt. For some time, the only words they exchanged were related to the game that seemed to go on forever. The sound of Alexander's voice startled them both.

'Perhaps we can play partners next?'

When Lucius glanced up, he noted Miss Ambrose standing next to his brother. Miss Cressida replied before he could. 'Certainly. Astrid and I can partner.'

'No,' Lucius snapped out. 'You know all her tells and tricks, as I know Alexander's. Let us make it more interesting. I'll pair with Miss Ambrose, and you may have my brother.'

Alexander laughed. 'We get no say then?'

'None.'

Once the pair were seated and the new game commenced, Lucius took the opportunity to mention to his partner a book he'd just finished reading that might be of use to her. 'It's not a thrilling read by any means, but there's quite a bit within its pages that I found useful with regards to crop rotation and livestock. It occurred to me you may also find something of value. I had not anticipated the pleasure of your ladies' company today, but if you'd like I can have it sent down to Red Fern Grange at your convenience.' He noted the quick look exchanged between the sisters.

Miss Ambrose smiled in her serene way. 'That's very kind. Thank you.'

'Yes,' added Miss Cressida, 'kind indeed. Perhaps, however, you might send the instructive tome here? Miss Harland is perpetually running out of reasons to walk out.'

He nodded his acquiescence and saw no reason to cause either sister embarrassment by openly challenging such a flimsy excuse as the one provided. Rather, he turned his mind to why they would make such a request. A single lady receiving a gift from a gentleman would be improper, but a book on estate management from one landowner to another and arranged in the open was hardly stretching the limits of propriety. Lucius couldn't like any of the conclusions at which he arrived. His attention was reclaimed by the game when his partner counted up her hand.

'And nobs makes seventeen.'

'Well done, Miss Ambrose! I believe we've the opportunity to veritably crush our opponents.' His smile was wide, his face animated by amusement, and had he not been focused on conspiring with his partner, he might have noticed the troubled look gracing the delicate features of the lady next to her. As it stood, whatever outward sign of the disquiet brewing within Miss Cressida had vanished by the time she spoke.

'You may, but we shan't make it easy for you.'

'I doubt you, Miss Cressida, make anything easy for anyone, including yourself.'

Lucius's bright eyes held her own, and he caught a flicker of something—uncertainty, understanding, bewilderment. It was gone before he could sort it out, but whatever it was, he thought about it long after he and Alexander had taken their leave.

9

'*D*o you mind if we go through the village?' Cressida asked her sister. 'I'd like some new laces for my boots. The left is bound to snap any day now.' She and Astrid were making their way home from the Smiths', where they went twice weekly to teach the youngest children reading and arithmetic.

Astrid agreed readily, and the two walked some distance in comfortable silence, for which Cressida was grateful. Her mind had been muddled since they took tea at the rectory, and she was struggling to parse out a clear reason for it. If she was entirely honest with herself, which she wasn't certain she could be, the confusing and often contradictory feelings had betrayed themselves weeks prior and only now were rattling around with enough force to disrupt her equanimity.

She was so distracted, she hadn't realised they'd reached the fringe of the main thoroughfare through Frambury, nor did she notice the middle-aged woman standing several feet before them wearing an expensive and elegant day dress and a hard, strained expression. It was Astrid's gentle touch that brought Cressida to the present moment, and she came to an abrupt halt when she saw what Astrid did.

The older woman made a hasty movement, and the young lady next to her put out a restraining hand, but the woman shook it off and approached with malice in her eyes, in her every movement. She came to a stop within a foot of Cressida.

'A cruel God he must be, to plague me with the likes of you.'

'I'm going about my business in the village where I was born and still reside. My presence can come as no great surprise, Lady Lisle.'

Lady Lisle scoffed. 'Yes, and how wonderful for *you* that *you* can still go about *your* business. There is no justice in this world.'

'Mama—' Miss Heaston interjected but swallowed whatever else she would have said when Lady Lisle turned her murderous look upon her daughter.

Cressida used the moment to steady her breathing and to hide her hands, which had begun to tremble a little, behind her back. 'I've done nothing wrong, ma'am.'

The older lady raked a disapproving look over Cressida, and the latter was sure that if they had been alone, the woman would have struck her.

'You may have fooled the bumptious people of this backwards village into thinking you a gentleman's daughter, but I know you for the conniving child you are and hope you don't know a moment's peace or happiness in the course of your sad little life.'

'That's enough,' Astrid said in a soft but firm voice. She threaded her arm through Cressida's and without another word steered them around the furious woman. When they were a little away, she said, 'Let us leave the laces for another day.'

Cressida gave her tacit consent by not protesting and bit the inside of her lip to keep her frustrated tears in check. Astrid said nothing else until they came round the bend that took them out of sight of the village.

'I'm sorry she's returned. We've been so fortunate until now to see nothing of her since her departure several years ago.'

That wasn't entirely true, and Cressida confessed to encountering Lady Lisle a year or so ago at the milliner's when she took Rebecca for some new ribbons. Shock and injury warred on Astrid's face.

'You never breathed a word—or Rebecca.'

Cressida released a heavy breath. 'No. Her ladyship waited until Rebecca was distracted at the back of the shop before she pounced. As for what she said, there seemed no reason to disclose the encounter. It was very much like the one when she left after the accident and the one today.'

'I hope you're not too affected by her words. They are designed to wound, but they come from a place of hurt—not a place of truth.'

Cressida didn't want to be upset by that woman's words, but even her resilience was threatened when faced with such direct, hateful language. She knew she wasn't responsible for the viscount's death, but his mother believed otherwise and made sure Cressida knew it. In the weeks immediately following his passing, Lady Lisle told anyone who would listen that Cressida had been to blame—and although most came to the very logical conclusion that such a thing was impossible, a few of his friends, and friends of the family, still looked at her as if wondering why she hadn't already been transported.

'Cressie?'

Cressida shook her head. 'That she can hold me in such contempt after what he did—tried to do—' The rest of the words caught in her throat and she swiped at the hot tears on her cheeks, silently admonishing herself for such a stupid display over such a stupid situation.

'But she doesn't know,' Astrid said, pulling Cressida a little closer to her side. 'And it would hardly matter if she did. She would only find it further proof of your naughtiness and take the opportunity to spread more vile tales.'

Her sister was right, of course. There were only two other people besides Cressida who knew the whole truth of what had transpired that fateful day—one was standing next to her, and the other was dead—and to tell anyone else would be to expose Cressida to rumour and ruin.

'I can't believe anyone ever thought the viscount a charming and amiable gentleman.' Her voice was laden with disgust, and she caught Astrid cringe at the harsh condemnation she doled out for herself.

'Many people still do.'

It was unfortunate but true. Tales illuminating James Heaston's true character began to circulate shortly before his death; the source Cressida never knew, but he had the foresight to die before most families were touched by his reckless and wild ways. Some saw him for what he was—a wastrel and scoundrel—others saw him for what he would be and have. His inheriting Tamarix one day was enough for them to turn a blind eye to his poor character.

'It's no matter,' Cressida replied in a rallying tone. 'Let us hope Lady Lisle's visit will be of short duration.' She forced a smile, but it dropped when she saw Astrid's doubtful countenance. 'What?'

'I don't believe it's chance that she's visiting so soon after the new lord installed himself at Tamarix Hall.'

'You think she means to make a match between him and one of her daughters?'

'It makes perfect sense, does it not?'

It did. The idea of Lord Windmere tied for life to such an odious woman should have brought a wicked smile to Cressida's face. It didn't, but she dismissed the odd turn of her thoughts without further consideration.

The days that followed passed in their usual quiet manner, with the added obstacle of a torrent of spring rain muddying the roads and preventing the sisters from walking out. From time to time, when they heard the door to their father's study open, they would scurry quiet as field mice down to the kitchen, desperate to maintain the tense peace that always felt a moment from fracturing if any one of them so much as looked at their father the wrong way.

Cressida, when she tired of fingering the old piano keys with listless interest, tossed herself onto the settee next to her eldest sister, who was wholly engrossed in a book.

'What absorbs the entirety of your attention, Astrid? You've not even made a single comment on my poor performance.'

Astrid's focus remained on the page in front of her for several moments before she raised her eyes to Cressida's, studying her sister with careful attention as she said, 'It's the one Lord Windmere recommended. Sophia brought it round the other day when we returned from the Smiths'. You were resting.'

Cressida worked to keep the surprise from her expression

and her voice. When she responded, it was in a measured tone. 'Ah, how kind.'

'He's right,' said Astrid, skimming the words on the page she'd just read. 'We should be alternating crops, at least on the easternmost field.'

'That's not what he said.' Her retort was sharp to her own ears, and Cressida wondered if her sister noticed.

'He's too civil to be so blunt. The notes he wrote in the margins are interesting as well.'

Cressida fought off the urge to examine his hand.

'I noted a few questions of my own I hope to put forward when we are next in company.

'You cannot mean to ask him for help,' Cressida said, outraged. It wasn't the idea of help that rankled her; it was the idea of *his* help, the idea that her dearest sister might mean to make a friend of the Corinthian.

Astrid replied with a look that brooked no argument. 'I mean to accept whatever help he's willing to offer. We'll drown here otherwise; we very nearly are already. Who else is there to help us? Before you make a rebuttal, which you no doubt desire to do, let me remind you that while he is not the first to offer assistance, he is the first to make good on his offer.'

She was right. They both knew it. The kindness extended to the Ambrose sisters stopped at the gates to Red Fern Grange. It was the way of things, Cressida knew. They were housed, fed, clothed by their father's whims—above all, they were their father's property, and who had the authority to challenge what was supported by law? She swallowed a bitter sigh, pulled some stockings out of a nearby basket, and fell into sullen silence.

A commotion in the hall sometime after the sun had passed

its halfway mark in the sky pulled all four ladies from their respective tasks, each pair of bright eyes looking around the room in silent question. Just as Astrid stood, her book set aside and her eyes alert with concern, a distinctly female and unfamiliar voice assailed their ears, growing louder as it approached the closed door.

'No need to introduce me, Mrs Hutchins. I've no intention of standing on ceremony with the girls.'

Cressida's heart thumped in her chest as she fixed her sight on the door just as it was thrown open to reveal a lanky, elegant woman in a deep green riding habit made of sturdy wool, with beautiful braiding halfway up the arms and gold epaulettes at the shoulders. Tucked under a jaunty little hat, from which a small plume of ostrich feathers curled and danced when the woman moved her head, were shining blond curls cropped short. She smiled immediately as she saw the young ladies perched, frozen in wonderment and worry. Clasping her hands to her chest, she said with real feeling and enthusiasm, 'What a charming picture you make—lovelier than I could ever have imagined. What fun we are going to have! Hutchins, we'll need tea and cakes. Do you have cakes? Well, if not, any sweetmeats will do. Now.'

The woman, after effectively dismissing the housekeeper, stepped further into the room. 'I won't pretend to know you from your appearance alone and therefore won't embarrass myself by guessing who's who, except you, Cressida dear—your hair is a dead giveaway.' The woman approached Cressida, cupping her cheek with tender care and studying her with watery eyes.

'Aunt Delia?' Cressida was struggling to reconcile this force of nature who had swept into their home with the woman she had met just once, at age five or six perhaps, and of whom she remembered very little except that she was beautiful and kind.

'Yes, darling, were you expecting someone else? Now, that's one down, three to go.'

Cressida and Astrid traded glances as Delia Wright, née Ambrose, known to them as Aunt Delia, passed from sister to sister, embracing and kissing them by turns as they offered up their names. 'Well, your father at least keeps a good cook,' she added, biting into a biscuit once the housekeeper had left.

It had been years since the Ambrose daughters had experienced any real familial affection except among themselves, and the lady's effusions stunned them all into an unmoving silence, broken only when Cressida said, 'I had not thought you'd come.'

'You and Astrid sent me a letter, pea-goose.'

'Yes.' Cressida blinked rapidly, still trying to comprehend the scene unfolding before her. 'But it's been an age.'

'The letter went to my home in London, which it would, of course. I can't comprehend how you are even in possession of that address, but as I've been abroad in India for more than a decade, it sat unopened these many months. It was luck—well, if one considers the death of one's husband a lucky thing—that it came to my possession when it did. I'd written of my return to London and had my mail held there, although closing the house in Bombay took longer than anticipated and the journey, of course, is no small endeavour. However, as soon as I read your letter, I told Murphy to repack my trunks because we were removing to Frambury post-haste.'

These disclosures were met with a chorus of questions. Aunt Delia did her best to answer them all: Mr Wright succumbed to fever earlier in the year; there was more than one way to mourn, but she would never be seen in black or grey as they did not complement her complexion; yes, she planned to remain 'as long as it takes.'

'As long as what takes?' asked Cora.

'The letter expressed concern for your futures, which is another way of saying none of you have come in the way of any eligible gentlemen—well, except you, dear,' Aunt Delia added, with a nod to Rebecca, 'you're far too young for marriage.'

'That's not quite—'

Aunt Delia interrupted Cressida's protestations. 'Yes, it is. The ladies most concerned for their futures are those unwed and without a grand inheritance upon which they may rely. You need not have used those words, but for what other reason could you have summoned me here? What you did not say, however, was why you, Cressida and Astrid, remain unwed or how I may be of use.'

Cressida frowned a little. She could hardly remember what they had put in the letter all those months ago.

'How many years have you girls been out now? Two? Three? It's too late to launch you in London this year, but perhaps Bath in the autumn or town next spring. New gowns are a must. No offence meant, and I imagine your dear mama educated you as young ladies ought to be, but I will need to see for myself how you conduct yourselves in public spaces.'

'We are not out, ma'am.' It was Astrid's quiet admission that put a full stop to their aunt's monologue.

'I beg your pardon? You must be'—Aunt Delia cocked her head to one side—'two- or three-and-twenty and Cressida only a year or two behind you.'

'I'm nearing twenty-one, and Astrid is two-and-twenty,' Cressida replied.

'You will need to give me more than that, child. How can it

be you're not out? No wonder you took such desperate measures. Goodness me.'

Cressida, seeing no point in withholding anything from their new and only ally, said with a steadiness at opposition to the frustration she felt with their situation, 'Father will not trouble himself to chaperone us. Even if he could be roused, there is no saying any families would issue invitations.'

'Well, that does put another shade on things.'

The sound of the drawing room door slamming open caused all five ladies within to start.

'What's the meaning of this?' The voice was loud but hollow, and the man in possession of it smaller in stature than would be expected of someone capable of producing such an ear-ringing noise.

'Ah,' Aunt Delia said, rising from her chair to approach her brother, who was several inches shorter than she and swaying precariously. The smell of brandy permeated the still air around him. 'Douglas, I won't pretend there is any joy to be found in seeing you.'

'Then you will be pleased to take yourself off forthwith, woman.'

'Always the man to think of only himself. I said there is no joy in seeing you. Your daughters are another matter.'

Cressida sat, eyes wide, lips parted in awe, and too absorbed in the tense scene unfolding to look anywhere else except at the heroine who'd swept into their life.

'Those chits are not your concern.'

'It rather appears they're not yours either. Short of removing yourself from this neighbourhood, and I imagine you too indolent to do as much, you have very little choice but to tolerate my presence. The extent, of course, is entirely dependent on yourself.'

'You will make no stay in this house, if that's what you're getting at.'

'No, on that we can agree. I've taken the lease on Blackbird Hall.'

'The Gunner residence?' Cressida asked. There had been no mention in town or from Sophia of the older couple relocating.

'Those charming people realised some time spent near the sea would be just the thing for their health.'

Cressida and Astrid looked at one another, eyebrows pulled to peaks.

Mr Ambrose shifted his weight from one foot to the other, swaying in his unsteady way. 'Get out of my house, Delia.'

Contrary to his demand, the lady showed no signs of moving, and for the first time in their lives, the Ambrose daughters watched in wonder as someone openly defied their father. 'No. Not until we come to some sort of understanding.'

Mr Ambrose grabbed the porcelain vase, which until that moment had lived on the buffet along the wall, and hurled it with a sad lack of force to the ground beside him before taking a menacing step forward, which his sister matched, to the surprise of all other occupants in the room.

Aunt Delia, with a look of patient indifference, said calmly, 'Your antics may frighten others into submission, Douglas, but after eighteen years under the same roof with you and nearly as many spent abroad, I find I'm immune to such petulant displays.'

He pulled his hand back to strike her but couldn't bring it up fast enough. Delia's own hand, clasped around her white kid gloves, swatted away his violent attempt, sending him teetering back towards the buffet. Cressida watched as he struggled to balance himself and for the first time realised how worn he looked; the lines of his face seemed deeper than they were even yesterday, his eyes hazy, his hair too wiry for his age.

'You forget how well I know you, brother.'

Mr Ambrose made fists at his side but no further attempt to harm his sister.

'Now,' she started, with an air of authority, 'I'll take on the charge of chaperoning the girls while I remain in the county.'

'No.'

'I haven't given you enough credit for the elasticity of your mind, for it is beyond my comprehension how you make sense of your contrary thinking. The girls are wasting their best years locked away.'

'And I wasted mine with a wife that bore me no son,' he scoffed, and for a brief moment, Cressida thought he might go so far as to spit on the floor in front of them. Idly, she wondered if he would have been so rough with *her* had she been born a boy.

'Yes,' Aunt Delia said, cutting into Cressida's thoughts. 'And if you'd like to do away with the reminders of such, it can easily be done by seeing them settled.'

The Ambrose sisters turned their eyes to their laps as their father looked them over with a gaze holding little else besides disgust. 'Not an ounce of anything worth marrying between 'em—no looks, no dowry—a waste of my time to pretend otherwise.'

Cressida's cheeks flamed, but she dared not look to see if her sisters were equally mortified by his false words. Only Astrid had a dowry in Red Fern Grange, that was true, but Cressida, perhaps biased, thought her sisters some of the loveliest girls she'd ever seen.

'So you have not, naturally. Chaperoning is a woman's work, and you need only continue as you always have.'

Outside somewhere a bird trilled, quick and shrill and so loud it felt as though it was circling overhead. It was the only sound heard for several minutes. In the end, Mr Ambrose grunted, hiccoughed, and said not a word further as he left the room, taking all the air with him but leaving behind something akin to hope.

10

The week after the tea at Mr Harland's, Lucius found himself once more in London at the request of his ageing solicitor who, according to his letter, 'needed but a day or two' to discuss several important matters pertaining to the family business and felt meeting face-to-face would be more expeditious than engaging in a series of letters, and more intelligible, too.

Lucius obliged Mr Hanks, believing himself happy for the respite, and when his carriage rolled up to his home on Brook Street, he had that familiar feeling of greeting an old friend. The large door swung open before he was put to the task of knocking.

'Impressive, even for you, Clarence,' he said, as he stripped off his hat and gloves and handed them to the waiting footman. 'I'm directly for my study. When Hanks presents himself,' he paused and consulted his pocket watch, 'within the hour, if I know the man, bring him to me. Oh, and some coffee would be just the thing.' His last words were thrown over his shoulder as he disappeared deeper into the house.

Clarence offered a perfunctory, 'Yes, sir,' although Lord Windmere was well beyond hearing.

Upon the desk were only a few letters, and those so recently arrived there was little point in forwarding them to Tamarix. They included a brief note from his Aunt Bea accepting his offer to visit him, with only a vague idea of when she would present herself. Underneath this was a thin missive with sharp, crisp creases and addressed in a flowing, feminine hand he recognised immediately.

He held it between thumb and forefinger, momentarily struck by the consciousness that he'd not dedicated a single thought to Lady Colchester since he departed London nearly two months previously. Being able to guess with fair accuracy what was contained within the pages, he rose, tossed the unopened letter in the fire, and set about replying to his aunt until Hanks was shown into the study a short while later.

The matter of import was more complex than urgent. Lucius had opened a regular school in addition to the lace school in his home county and had been in the process of continuously improving the working conditions for the five hundred or so labourers, but growing and bettering the business was not without its own set of complications and troubles. After two full days and half of another locked away, Hanks leaving only to sleep in his own bed, everything was settled.

After he'd thanked Hanks and seen the long-suffering solicitor out, Lucius spent an hour in the library thumbing through his favourite book of poems until every line brought to mind a pair of clear green eyes and he set it aside in search of more distracting entertainment. He donned his hat and gloves and stepped out, taking two rights, and before long, finding himself gaining easy admittance to number ten in Berkeley Square.

He'd informed no one besides his staff of his brief return and savoured the look of shock upon Lord Dane's face as he strode into the book room at the back of the house.

'Luci! Oh, I beg your pardon,' Dane corrected with a twinkle in his eye as he rose to greet one of his oldest friends with a bow. 'My Lord Windmere.'

'Not you too, Dane.'

'Certainly me. What good fortune for me, knowing you these last twenty or more years. I may impose upon you as much as I'd like and put the connection to use as often as I open my mouth without any fear of losing it. Brandy?'

Lucius nodded through his laughter. The two had met at Eton several lifetimes ago. And Francis Coventry, having inherited his earldom at the tender age of six, had often been the only thing that kept Lucius tethered to the world during his dark years. After Lucius left school, Dane had kept up a correspondence, often sending one letter before another had its reply. Sometimes it was practical, measured advice, sometimes nothing more than a retelling of an anecdote Dane had heard or the stupid antics in which he participated.

Taking a sip of his brandy and watching his friend from over the rim of the glass, Lucius wondered if Dane had any idea how much those letters mattered. Certainly he must have some little idea; a young man in school never took time to write as Dane did. Lucius took another longer swallow to wash away the mawkish sentiments that threatened to over-power him.

'Are you engaged this evening?' Dane asked.

'Not at all. The knocker's off, and I've plans to return to Tamarix on the morrow.'

'Then say you will dine with us tonight and remain for the musicale after. Almeria would be delighted to have you.'

A grin touched Lucius's lips. 'Scoundrel.'

'Dinner is at eight, but come as early as you please—you may go home, change, and bring yourself right back.'

Lucius didn't return so fast as that, but he was once more ascending the steps of number ten promptly at six in response to the directive that had arrived at Brook Street only minutes after he himself did:

You will be on my doorstep at 6 p.m. or I will be on yours one minute past.

- A

'Your servant, ma'am,' he said, as he entered the salon where Lord and Lady Dane were seated.

Lucius adored Dane's wife. The couple had married young, even before Lord Dane was of age, and over the years she'd come to be a sister of sorts to Lucius. Almeria jumped from her place, meeting him in the middle of the room and kissing his cheek even as she questioned the length of his locks, wondered if he kept a good cook at Tamarix because she thought his coat not quite so fitted as she remembered, and generally pulled his person apart as any assessing sister might.

'Tell me about the property. Are you nearly ready for guests? The season is so flat this year without you here to provide gossip.'

He answered all her questions with impressive patience, teased her mercilessly about anything and everything, and did so without realising how many times he mentioned Miss Cres-

THE RAKE OF TAMARIX HALL

sida or noticing the subtle looks exchanged between husband and wife.

The rest of the evening passed as expected with one notable exception. He came face to face with Miss Dench at the musicale, which in and of itself was nothing to wonder at as she was a cousin of Lady Dane's and it was how Alexander and the young lady first met. It was the skittish way Miss Dench addressed Lucius and her stilted request that he convey her well wishes to his brother that struck him as exceedingly unusual. Lucius hadn't heard his brother mention the lady in some time but was under the assumption they were exchanging letters with her father's permission, which was not so uncommon for a couple approaching an understanding.

By the following day, Lucius felt perhaps he was so caught up in his own affairs he had overlooked something of importance, and when he returned to Tamarix, he sought out Alexander before embarking on any other task and discovered his brother reading in the conservatory.

'You look rather content.'

'Should I be otherwise?' Alexander countered, looking up from his book.

'I've been wondering.'

At this point, Alexander closed his book and sat up a little straighter, his eyes a little sharper. 'You're speaking in riddles, Luci.'

'I am always delighted with your company, for however long you wish to bestow it, but I admit to feeling some surprise that you've neither made for Branford nor for London.'

'Are you kicking me out?'

Lucius studied his brother in measured silence, wondering how far and how hard to push. 'Never. Only I imagined after you saw me settled here that you would be anxious to settle your own affairs with Miss Dench.'

'You've no need of me to see you *settled.*'

The brothers entered into a staring contest, each waiting for the other to speak. Lucius wore his mask of relative indifference, knowing it would only be another minute or so before his brother cracked. Alexander shifted in his seat and let out an impatient huff.

'Dash it, Luci! What? What is it you're wishing I'd say? You may as well tell me so we can complete this ridiculous exchange and I can return to my book, which, by the by, I was enjoying until you appeared.'

'No need to be peevish, Alexander. It occurred to me I had not heard you speak of your Miss Dench in recent weeks, and I am only wondering when I can expect an announcement.'

Alexander's eyes narrowed, and Lucius noticed his brother's jaw twitch. 'There will be no announcement, but I expect you already came to such a conclusion.'

'I had wondered,' Lucius admitted. 'You need not say more if you dislike the idea.'

The younger Anselme shook his head. They weren't in the habit of keeping things from one another, and that Alexander had held this particular bit of information close for so long had given Lucius some idea of the disarray he must be sorting through in his mind. 'You did a kind thing, giving me Branford. Only I hadn't realised the full extent of my own ignorant bliss before then.'

Lucius didn't take his brother's meaning and looked a question at him.

'You know, I told myself her parents wouldn't countenance our match because I hadn't enough to offer her, enough to keep her in the style in which she's been accustomed all her life.'

'That's not quite true,' Lucius replied, keeping his tone mild and calm despite the little offence he took at such an absurd statement. Alexander had been left a neat sum upon the death of their mama, although it was not so great that he could afford to purchase an estate outright. He would always have had to lease someone else's lands, and for men like Mr Dench, whose family had held the same seat nearly two hundred years, the quality of being a leaseholder wasn't something easily overlooked. Lucius thought Miss Dench perfectly unexceptionable, but he struggled to find something to appreciate in men like her father.

'Yes, yes.' Alexander waved away the interjection. 'I know I could keep a carriage and servants, and all the generally expected trappings of comfort. But Miss Dench comes from an old family. She could marry a title if she pleases.'

Lucius raised his eyebrows a little, beginning to feel fatigued with the conversation. He failed to grasp whatever problem was separating the pair, now that Alexander was himself part of the landed gentry, and wondered if his brother would come to the point before dinner was announced. He was debating between asking Alexander directly and checking his watch and excusing himself when Alexander confessed to having seen Miss Dench nearly as soon as Lucius told him Branford would be his.

'"Just as it should be. Your brother can no longer have use for it now that he's finally the marquess," is what she said. "Finally,"' Alexander repeated.

Lucius hid his disgust by drawing in a slow, steady breath.

'Her mama keeps up with all the gossip. And, according to Miss Dench, that lady said some time ago that if they were patient, surely you would do something for your poor brother when you came into the title. So you see, Luci, it wasn't that I didn't have enough, simply that they wanted more.'

'I see.' Lucius wasn't as surprised by this revelation as his brother. In fact, he wasn't surprised at all. Avarice was as common in the higher circles of society as ostrich feathers, turbans, and gambling debts.

'I could never marry a woman like that, a woman always wanting more. But you're right about one thing—it's past time for me to set up house at Branford.'

Lucius worked to stay engaged in the conversation, but he hadn't realised until the precise moment his brother said he wouldn't marry Miss Dench how much hope he'd stored up in just that probability—how much he depended upon that expectation. Lucius never wanted to burden his brother, but had Alexander married Miss Dench and set up a nursery, it was very possible that there would have been a nephew whom Lucius could've taken under his wing. That wouldn't negate the possibility of an unforeseen accident of some sort cutting Lucius's life much too short, but there would have been another who could manage the estate, at least alongside Alexander, if not entirely. Alexander's marriage and future children had been, Lucius realised, his own last hope of avoiding matrimony.

11

*S*ix days after the arrival of Aunt Delia, that fine lady attended all four of her nieces through the charming high street of Frambury with one specific goal. 'A new day dress for each of you, and ballgowns as well—except for you, child,' she said with a consoling pat on Rebecca's arm. 'You may, however, have a second day dress, or something else altogether if you'd prefer.'

Astrid protested, as did Cressida; it was insupportable for their aunt to purchase eight new gowns—eight!—when the ones the girls had were perfectly serviceable, if a little worn and a little out of the current style.

'Have you dresses appropriate for a ball?' Aunt Delia asked, despite the challenge in her smile saying she knew very well they did not.

'We have no use for them.' Cressida set her lips in a mulish line.

'You *had* no use for them. Any young lady with even the least expectation of attending a private or public ball ought to have one appropriate dress. Did you not mention neighbours expecting visitors? Perhaps they will honour their guests with such an evening. Or I shall host one. I dearly loved doing so in India.'

'You?' Cressida's eyes flickered to her sisters', which were filled with varying degrees of excitement and wonder.

Aunt Delia smiled as she ushered them into a shop to look at fabrics. 'Close your mouth, dear.'

Cressida began on another question but faltered halfway through and broke off in some confusion, conscious of the offence she was about to give. Rebecca spoke up in the absence of a new topic, doling out the affront Cressida had narrowly avoided. 'But, Aunt, are not friends and acquaintances required to host a ball? You have neither here.'

Before any of her elder sisters could reprimand her, Aunt Delia proffered her own reply. 'Your sister put an abrupt end to her inquiry upon the realisation that pursuing it must give injury. You, dear, spared her further embarrassment by saving it for yourself.' It was a capital set-down, and Cressida felt guilty for enjoying it and for not doing more to curb Rebecca's wild tongue. Cressida knew herself to be more outspoken, more direct than was ladylike or polite, and it was little wonder her sister was following her poor example. Her guilt increased when she noticed Rebecca's red cheeks and the quiver of her lip that suggested she was fighting back tears.

'It's all right.' Aunt Delia took Rebecca's hand in her own and gave it a squeeze. 'You're a very prettily behaved girl, you just need a bit of polishing. You all do,' she added with an appraising look that swept over them. 'I suspect being involved in ball preparations and general hosting responsibilities wouldn't go amiss either.'

The girls said nothing because there was nothing to say. They elder two learned economy and the basics of running a household from their mama, but the other responsibilities that often fell to the mistress of the house became irrelevant when their mother became ill.

'Very true, ma'am,' replied Astrid, 'and you are kind to take such an interest in us.'

'Oh!' Cora's bright exclamation pulled the ladies' attention. 'Cressie, only think how this would bring out the green of your eyes. It's the colour of the phlox blooming off the lane near the Harlands', only lighter even.'

Cressida walked to where her sister stood and ran the silky material through her fingers. It was the faintest shade of lavender she'd ever seen. 'It's far too fine.' The other ladies had wandered off into deeper corners of the shop, but she was still admiring the fabric, imagining what it would be like to own a dress so lovely, to dance in a dress so lovely, to dance at all, when the young girl who worked in the shop came over and pulled it down from the shelf at Aunt Delia's request.

A fortnight after her arrival, Aunt Delia had, in addition to procuring new dresses for her nieces and embarking on little lessons with them, secured several invitations for herself and 'her girls', as the local populace were quickly coming to think of the Ambrose sisters. The general curiosity in a vibrant newcomer and unabashed interest in seeing the elder two of the sisters move about in society was more than enough to open drawing room doors.

'For my part,' stated Mrs Peregrine to Mrs Hobbs while at a musicale some weeks after Aunt Delia's arrival, 'I think nothing could be better for those dears.'

Cressida heard the comment as she passed behind the pair and was inclined to agree, although she suspected some matrons preferred less competition for their own daughters, even if the competition had comparatively little to offer a potential suitor. The wry thought withered when, upon scanning the room, her eyes alighted on Lady Lisle. The only outward sign of displeasure was a quick pinch of her lips. There were at least a dozen families packed into a space better suited for half that number, however, and Cressida decided that if both were determined to avoid the other, they could do so very easily.

And determined she was. The novelty of the evening, the unparalleled joy to be found in her first night away from her father, from Red Fern Grange, and among friends she only saw while walking in town or at the Harlands' monthly card party, was such that even the presence of Lord Windmere could not spoil it. Even after the marquess sought an introduction to Aunt Delia and complimented Cressida on her high looks, she could do little else besides think him a teasing, provoking man and said as much.

'Then I am all at fault for the delivery of my compliment, as it stems from genuine feeling.'

'You,' she replied, her voice low to keep the words between them, 'are incapable of genuine feeling.' A shadow of something flitted across his handsome face—hurt maybe—and for a moment she felt guilty for speaking such harsh words.

'I'm sorry you should think so.'

'Are you?'

'Sorry? Quite—but not at all surprised. We often react most strongly to those characteristics in others we see most in ourselves.'

Her mouth dropped open a little, but he went away in the next moment, leaving no space for a rejoinder. She was still watching his back as he crossed the room when a familiar and most unwelcome voice whispered over her shoulder, 'Shall I bring you rope to facilitate the climb?'

Cressida turned, settling her expression into one of blank composure. 'I beg your pardon, my lady, but I don't take your meaning.' She did, of course, and had Lady Lisle been someone else altogether, Cressida may have appreciated the open and unforgiving insult.

'My poor James may have been taken in by you, young, trusting boy that he was, but that gentleman will not. A piece of advice if I may.' Without waiting for agreement, the lady continued, 'A country mouse such as yourself has no business aiming so high. You are lucky to be here at all. Set your sights on the rector from Chilternfield, or perhaps a rich merchant if you are feeling ambitious.'

With a smile pinned to her face, Cressida said, 'When I have need of your opinion, I'll most certainly seek it out. Until then, let us preserve our dignity through decided silence.'

Lady Lisle looked as though she had sucked a lemon but without another word returned to her daughters, who, Cressida noted, were shortly brought round to the side of the room where Lord Windmere stood.

Under the pretence of an engaging conversation with Miss Tambor, Cressida watched the interaction from the periphery of her vision, ignoring the flutter of satisfaction that coursed through her when, after a brief conversation in which each party failed to give even the appearance of interest in the other, Lord Windmere strode away to join his brother, who was in conversation with Aunt Delia.

How Cressida found herself drifting towards the little group was entirely beyond her, but as she approached, she thought with no little shame that if her aunt had been privy to the way she'd spoken to Lord Windmere earlier, the dear woman would be horrified. Cressida knew she was at times insolent, saying things that were better left unsaid in polite company, and now to a man far above her station, but until Aunt Delia had presented herself, none of it mattered. What use had Cressida, or any of the Ambrose sisters, for society manners when they had existed only on the fringes? Now, she felt the sting of mortification on her cheeks and agitation swell in her breast. Lady Lisle's accusation that Cressida was setting her cap at him only compounded both.

'Your sister has just informed me that this is your first time out in local society,' Mr Anselme said, addressing Cressida when she approached. She acknowledged the truth of it. 'And how are you enjoying yourself? Does the evening exceed your expectations?'

'Very much, sir, but what an odious creature I would be if I was above being pleased, if not by the company, then at least by the novelty of new experience.'

Mr Anselme's lips turned up in a smile, and she returned one of her own, pleased with his easy manners. 'You cannot convince me of your being odious in any circumstances, but I know better than to argue with a lady.' His eyes slipped briefly to his brother as he said so. 'I will only add that novelty, as you put it, agrees with both you and your sister.'

Astrid flushed prettily and dropped her eyes, receiving this as any well-bred lady ought. Cressida, however, found herself once more the target of Lord Windmere.

'Are you now more inclined to take my words as they were meant?' His lips were quirked up at the corners, but his eyes held an indecipherable expression she was trying to parse out as he continued. 'Because Miss Ambrose looks very well indeed, particularly in yellow, but you, Miss Cressida, I don't think I've ever seen a young lady look so lovely as you do in this moment.'

She couldn't mistake the warmth in his voice, ignore the

steady, penetrating look he pinned upon her, or prevent the bloom of pink rising from the low neckline of her dress out over the tips of her ears and to the roots of her hair. With a vague reply, she excused herself and stepped outside in a futile attempt to regain her equanimity and cool the warmth radiating within. But even the air and its dependable spring chill weren't enough. That feverish feeling remained, even as she tossed and turned in her bed long into the night.

12

*L*ucius heard the rap of his aunt's walking stick several seconds before Yates opened the door to the study and ushered the compact elderly woman in.

She took one step over the threshold, hardly leaving enough space for Yates to pull the door closed as he exited, cast an appraising eye over the drapes, the chairs, the ugly ornamental urn upon the mantelshelf, and said, 'How you're able to get an ounce of work done in such appalling surroundings exceeds my capacity for understanding, which I believe to be exceptional.'

Lucius had come round the desk to greet her and kissed her cheek through his chuckle. 'My rooms remain at the bottom of a rather lengthy list.'

'You're too kind by half, my boy,' she replied, a note of censure in her voice, which had roughened a bit with age.

Lucius shook his head and ignored the comment, a common refrain where his aunt was concerned. 'How long may I depend upon your company, ma'am?'

'The answer is entirely dependent on how you mean to entertain me. At least a fortnight, I suppose, to rest the horses and myself.'

'The journey is hardly a full day of travel, even by carriage. In summer, you could leave Branford and arrive at Tamarix with plenty of light on either side,' he said reprovingly, mischief sparking in his eyes.

'By the by, Lucius, do you know if your brother prefers my returning to town on a permanent basis?' Upon her husband's death, Aunt Bea had been given lifetime rights to their house in town. The country manor where they had resided together had gone to her husband's son from a previous marriage. In the years since Lucius took over Branford, she spent most of her time in that property's dower house.

'You may ask him for yourself. He remains here.'

When his aunt lifted a thin grey eyebrow, he said in dreadful dramatic accents, 'Indeed.' As he moved to pour her a glass of Madeira, he added, 'He and I have not touched upon the topic, but I thought to offer you the dower house here if you'd like it. I suppose you can have both if Alexander doesn't protest your claim to the other.'

She took the glass from his hand, eyeing him over its rim. 'I'll withhold a decision until I see what this part of the country can offer. The pretty little village was better equipped than I expected and larger compared to the one nearest Branford. What are your neighbours like? Toadeaters? Heathens? Hoydens?'

'You absurd creature. They are by and large perfectly amiable—much like our neighbours at Branford. You may even find a friend or two among them.' She and Mrs Peregrine would be fast friends. 'Now come,' he said, removing the glass from her hand and placing it on the tray next to the decanter before offering her his arm. 'I'll take you to your room myself. You'll want to rest and plan the interrogation you no doubt mean to take place at dinner.'

His Aunt Bea cackled but made no move to deny the accusation, and indeed, by the time he'd finished the duckling served in the second course, Lucius felt like a boy of sixteen again.

Several weeks after the death of Lucius and Alexander's father, Aunt Bea had turned up at Branford. Lucius had not asked her to—it hadn't occurred to him to do such a thing—but she'd veritably stormed the front door, enough luggage piled high on a second carriage to suggest she meant to stay a while, and declared her intention of seeing things put right, because, in her words, 'What does a boy of two-and-twenty know besides where the good liquor is hidden or how to get out of a scrape?' She'd asked hundreds of questions about the estate, the tenants, the servants, the accounts, deliveries, vendors, investments, the lace business; she'd asked about the silver inventory, his mother's extensive jewellery collection, how often the linens were replaced, and what he would do if one servant accused another of theft or some other crime.

In short, she'd shown Lucius how little he knew about the estate and how ill-prepared he was to manage it on his own. There were people who would know the answers to these questions, of course—a steward, a cook, a housekeeper—but no piece of information pertaining to an estate, she told him, was beneath an estate holder. He had tried once to thank her, but she waved his words away and told him not to be a goose-cap. Instead, when she'd announced her plans to return to London, he'd taken her to the dower house, shown her the improvements he had made in secret, and invited her to remain.

'I hadn't intended to remain longer than a month, but perhaps I ought to stay on through summer to act as hostess for a party...The Levins, Russells, Harpers, Hammersmiths.' She paused to sip her wine and consider her two nephews.

'Will the sons be invited or only the daughters?'

'We can't very well exclude the sons if they remain at home, but besides the Russell boy, the others are rather whey-faced, do not you think? No doubt their mamas will sort out the situation themselves and dispatch the young men if need be.'

Lucius felt the prickles of irritation intensify the longer he remained at the table. 'There is no need. I have not the least intention of inviting any families with single daughters to marry off to be guests under my roof. No doubt one would find the keys to my chambers, and by dawn I'd find myself engaged to half a dozen ladies or more.'

His aunt looked at him through unamused eyes, but his brother's glimmered with mirth. Lucius made a mental note to wring his brother's neck later for not taking at least some of the attention off him. When she opened her mouth to protest, he cut her off. 'No, no more. You know my feelings on the topic. If your plan is to browbeat me for the duration of your stay, I'll have your carriage brought round at first light.'

There was a full minute of silence before she said, 'Fine.' She allowed other topics of conversation to be discussed and dispensed with before bringing forward another unpalatable subject. 'I heard *that* woman is here.'

'Lady Lisle is staying with a Mrs Davies. Two of her daughters as well.'

'Has she been to see you?'

He nodded once, and she gave a derisive little grunt.

'She lived a large portion of her life in this village. It is not so surprising for her to return to visit friends. Poor manners, as we know, are often offset by breeding and wealth—you yourself are perhaps an example.' He compressed his lips to hide a smile.

Although all three retired early, Lucius remained awake until his candle guttered in its holder, thinking of everything and of nothing in particular all at once. Still, when the sun began to rise and the blackness of his room began to give way to early-morning grey, despite his sleepless night, he rose and escaped for a solitary ride.

He set off with no determined direction in mind and was a little startled to find himself taking Helios up the back of Dryce Hill. The two arrived at the top just in time to catch sight of a figure in a dark green cape retreating down the other side. Lucius knew from the glint of brilliant yellow-white hair peeking out of the hood that it was Miss Cressida, and even as he wondered if she'd started down at the sound of someone coming up, he was urging his horse forward. Her steps quickened, and only then did he realise for all she knew he was a stranger at her back.

'Miss Cressida!'

She halted at his call but didn't turn, remaining still until he brought Helios around to face her and dismounted.

'You thought to outrun a man on horseback?' he asked, a teasing lilt to his voice.

Annoyance flashed in her eyes. 'Should I have waited and simply allowed myself to be abducted or accosted?'

'In Frambury? The village is hardly home to lechers and rapists.'

A shadow swept over her face, like a cloud crossing the

sun, and her expression shuttered. She bobbed a shallow curtsey and turned to continue down the hill.

'You cannot possibly think I'd let you walk alone after your suggestion that all manner of danger is lurking behind every tree and hedgerow,' he said, falling into step beside her.

She made no reply, but he heard her exhale, no doubt debating whether silence or a set-down was the best way to deal with her unwanted companion. When she at last spoke, he was taken aback by her words.

'Why did you give my sister that book?'

'To be helpful, or so I hope.'

'Why?'

He studied her profile, noting the stubborn set of her jaw, the taut line drawn by her lips, and he could feel her straining against something he couldn't see or feel or fix. He had thought, naturally, to needle her a little, as she was so fond of provoking him. But now they weren't in a drawing room or salon, or surrounded by people or things offering an easy escape—it was just the two of them, blades of grass wet with morning dew attaching themselves to their boots, the first light of the day bestowing a celestial glow on Miss Cressida.

'I was quite young when Branford Park became mine. My father had gone, my mother not long before him, and the estate, along with Alexander, became my responsibility. My father, who in his life had been a wonderful parent and estate owner, was, near his end, too consumed with his own grief to guide me as he ought. It was a challenging time, and there were days, more than I could ever count, when I simply wished the ground would open and swallow me whole.' Lucius could feel Miss Cressida's eyes on him now, but he couldn't face her as he made his confession, as he disclosed feelings that had always lived only in his head.

'The truth is, I don't know what would have become of me, of my family home, of my brother, if there hadn't been anyone to help me.'

He chanced a glimpse in her direction and thought she looked a little bewildered, which was not so very shocking. There were things that pained him to think of and so he never gave voice to them, as if keeping everything closed up tight inside might somehow suffocate the worst of his aches and pain and grief.

She continued for a time in her silence, her mouth turned down a little, and he was just beginning to wonder if he'd made a mistake in exposing himself in such a way, when she said, 'Red Fern Grange was my mother's dowry and is now Astrid's, because there was no son. Although you've no acquaintance with my father, sir, you can very likely surmise his feelings on such a thing. He has done just enough to keep a good table and to afford himself new waistcoats and boots and brandy, but letting it slowly fall to pieces is perhaps his little bit of revenge. He's never cared much for women, you see.'

She said this as if it clarified the entirety of her situation, but it left Lucius with more questions than answers, and he struggled against the rising anger he felt at such an indolent, selfish man. He broached the one subject he'd been curious about almost since stepping foot in Frambury. 'And your mama?'

Miss Cressida looked everywhere but at him before answering, 'An angel. How she ever—' She broke off with a shake of her head, although Lucius suspected he knew how she would finish her thought. 'My mama hadn't much of a head for these kinds of things, but she did what she could and applied herself to reading the books in the little library that she felt could be of use. My father saw her doing so once, ordered a fire—it was the middle of summer, I remember—and burned them all.'

Her voice cracked, and he watched as she turned her head a little away from him. Something about the movement, about her desire to hide herself from him, caused a swell of agitation within him—and it was with disconcerting clarity he understood why: his own desire to comfort her.

13

It had been years since Cressida had felt scared walking alone—since she wouldn't step out without Astrid or Sophia at her side—but when she felt the pounding of horse hooves underneath her feet and heard them at her back only a moment later, her skin broke out in a cold sweat and she quelled the urge to run, knowing there was no shelter and no escape.

The impossibility of it being the viscount mattered not. Her mind panicked; her limbs trembled with fear. Her relief when she heard Lord Windmere's voice, carried to her by the wind, was palpable: her shoulders dropped, her jaw unclenched, her limbs, although still uneasy, no longer shook with violence. Notorious rake, eavesdropper, pebble in her boot—he was a lot of things, but she had never felt afraid of him. The thought gave her pause as she stood waiting for his approach.

He escorted her home, or at least as close as she allowed him. When they were just within view of the Grange, she refused to take another step with him beside her. At first he threatened to simply wait her out, claiming he could stand in one spot at least as long as she herself could, but when she began to walk in the direction from which they came, he relented with a promise not to catch her up. Instead, he waited from that spot to see her safely inside from a distance.

She didn't need to turn back to know he was watching, keeping his word. It was only after she'd disappeared round the corner to enter through the kitchen that she dipped and angled her head just enough to see from her periphery that he'd mounted his horse and was only then turning in the direction of Tamarix.

His presence had discomfited her. First his turning up as he did, and then by sharing such a confidence. She had thought by now she was rather an expert in his vexatious expressions and mannerisms, but in all their interactions she had never seen him like that—with his countenance so open and a quiver of vulnerability in his voice. He had revealed a part of himself she wished he hadn't—a part that made him more human.

This unguarded moment was occupying all of her thoughts when the sound of her name, called in a thick, watery sort of voice, brought her to a tense halt. There was no clock for her to consult, but she imagined the morning hour had yet to reach eight, and her father rarely rose before ten on his best days. He called out to her again, and this time she worked her face into a neutral expression as she pushed the half-open door to his study. Cressida looked at him, taking in his rumpled cravat, the coat on the back of his chair the same he'd worn the day prior, and the empty decanter on the edge of the desk. He had not risen early—he had yet to retire.

'Yes, Father?' She was proud of how steady her voice sounded. No matter how often she told herself there was nothing to fear from him, dread wrapped itself around her bones whenever she neared him. He hadn't raised a hand to her in some time, but she was always acutely aware of his temper, of the damage he could do if the fancy struck him. She was helpless to prevent it, and they both knew it.

In the past, the housekeeper would bring her a cold compress or a plaster and always some words of excuse. 'He's long suffered the disappointment of having only daughters. That's quite a blow, and men are such tetchy creatures, you know.' Sometimes it was more so, 'Perhaps if miss could just think upon her own behaviours.' And her sisters, what could they do—what would she want them to do? Nothing, was of course the answer to both questions. Once, Astrid had cried out in protest, and the back of their father's hand had found her cheek as well. Cressida had felt so guilty she'd made all her sisters promise never to be so stupid again.

'I'll have no baggage in this house. I made that mistake with your mother.'

Cressida sucked in a breath at the insinuation. 'I beg your pardon?'

Mr Ambrose lolled his head towards the window. 'That man.'

'Lord Windmere, sir. He came upon me as I walked home and saw me here safely.'

Far from pacifying her father or assuring him of the marquess's gallantry, this explanation was rewarded with a scoff. Her father's eyes narrowed in contemptuous humour. 'You're a bigger fool than even she was. One whiff, the barest hint, girl, and you'll be quite dependent on him for a cottage in some out of the way part of the country.'

Cressida's skin burned and itched in discomfort. She stammered a little as she attempted to reply, 'I'm not—there's no—it's not—'

For a moment his gaze appeared almost lucid as he

measured the truth of her sputtered words. 'Ay, and there better not be, if you know what's good for you. I'll have no one thinking I've raised girls with loose morals.'

She blinked back her tears, refusing to give him the satisfaction, and swallowed down a retort on how little he'd participated in the raising of her and her sisters. She had often wondered why, if he felt such animosity towards her, he didn't send her away or make it known that her paternity was questionable. In that moment, like a ray of sun forcing its way through interminable cloud cover, it became clear. There were few things Mr Ambrose cared about, but he saw the behaviour of his wife and daughters as a reflection on him. That people should see him as a man unable to control the women in his life was insupportable. Exposing her meant exposing himself as a cuckold.

Cressida remained silent, feeling there wasn't anything she could say that wouldn't further stoke his ire.

'Go, and send Kemp to me,' he added, eyeing the decanter.

She acknowledged the request and escaped as quickly as she could without it being obvious. Astrid was no longer in their shared room, which suited Cressida and her disturbed mind perfectly well. She could focus on nothing and was grateful for the silence as she marched herself over to the little seat in the window. She drew her knees up and rested her chin upon them, staring out over the mild landscape of her home county, Dryce Hill rising at a distance in the background. She was fatigued by her father's harsh words, by ever-present worry for her and her sisters' futures, fatigued from carrying a secret that sometimes weighed on her like rocks in her pockets.

It had been a Tuesday in November when her mother made the confession. The girls had been taking turns watching over their mama, and Cressida had hardly filled the chair left warm by Astrid when Mrs Ambrose reached a shaky hand towards her second daughter. The faint pressure on her fingers was just enough to alert Cressida, to signify something was coming, although she could never have guessed what. She could recall everything about that moment: the oppressive heat from the fire, the smell of sick and decay, the look in her mother's eyes —apprehension, remorse, desperation.

There was no strength left in her mother for flowery speeches or lengthy explanations, and so she went right to the heart of the matter. Mr Ambrose had had guests, a baron he knew from Oxford and the man's wife, breaking their journey on the way to Tunbridge Wells. The last night of their stay, the man came to Mrs Ambrose's chamber and forced himself upon her. It was in this position Mr Ambrose found them. It was possible that man was Cressida's father, but there was no way to know for certain.

Until that moment, Cressida had spent her life wondering why her father seemed to have so marked a dislike of her. She spent countless nights crying into her pillow, thinking up ways to earn his love while Astrid rubbed her back. She was still young enough then to believe such a thing possible. She picked him flowers, stitched his initials into handkerchiefs, wrote him little poems. Whatever it was, he tossed it into the fire while she watched.

Her mother tried to lift a hand to Cressida's face. Cressida bowed and pressed her cheek to her mother's palm, holding it there and savouring the warmth, knowing moments like those were quickly coming to an end.

'I'm sorry,' her mother croaked out, and Cressida had no need to ask for what. Bearing children had been hard on her. She'd become increasingly weak with each one, making her susceptible to every illness imaginable until one finally claimed her life. Cressida knew the apology was for not protecting her—doing so was an impossibility, and they both knew as much.

She hadn't intended to keep the secret from her eldest sister, but she was unsure how to impart such news and each day that passed only made it harder, until so much time had lapsed that sharing her secret felt like an impossibility. Instead, she carried it alone. And now it was just one of the many things she could feel pulling her apart from the inside out.

In this vein, March became April, and her aunt, having made friends with many of the local families, firmly planted herself on the social ladder by hosting a ball. Aunt Delia had readied the girls for the event by engaging all of them in the preparations; doling out lessons on receiving guests, making polite conversation, and general deportment; and bringing in a dancing master for them. By the night of the ball, Cressida was as relieved to be free from the planning of it as she was excited to partake in the enjoyment of the evening.

'I own I'm quite relieved that my aunt forced these new dresses upon us,' Astrid remarked in a low voice, as they stood in the receiving line with Aunt Delia. Their new dresses were the height of fashion and the loveliest thing either owned. Astrid had selected a soft pink that brought out the natural bloom on her cheeks and had adorned her dress with ruffles and rosettes, in contrast to the simpler design of her sister's, which had an open robe of airy white gauze embroidered with delicate silver leaves on the bodice.

As her sister spoke, Cressida ran the fine pale lavender satin between her thumb and index finger, as if she could feel it through the fabric of her gloves, and murmured her agreement, but she was too distracted by Lord Windmere's approach to say anything more.

He cut a fine figure; it was appalling, really, how well he looked in full evening dress. His white silk cravat set off the sculpted plains of his handsome face and the dark umber of his hair. His deep blue coat showed the perfect taper of his broad chest to his defined waist. And his satin knee breeches refused to give an inch on his muscular thighs. With effort, she directed her eyes back to the Hobbses, who were standing before her.

She had seen less of his lordship the preceding weeks than she had grown accustomed, and when they had been in company, she thought him rather more distant than usual and not as eager to spar with her. She wondered, not for the first time, if he regretted taking her into his confidence during their morning walk. When he appeared in front of the little group, she searched for any sign of discomfort or shame but saw none. His visage was intent, and she discovered him returning her stare in an equally considering way. She ignored the palpitation in her chest and tried to focus as her aunt expressed her hope that Mr Anselme had had an uneventful journey to Branford Park the week before. This was confirmed by Lord Windmere, who then moved deeper into the ballroom and out of Cressida's sight.

She opened the dancing with one of Sophia's brothers and saw with some displeasure that Astrid was standing across from Mr St John. That gentleman was still very much on the hunt for a wife, and the attention he paid Astrid when in company, especially since she was now out, had not gone unnoticed by Cressida. She had been reluctant to broach the sensitive subject a second time, but with an inward sigh suspected she would soon be required to do so.

The first set rolled into the next and the evening was nearly half gone when Cressida paused long enough to take refreshment and compliment her aunt on a perfect evening, which it was, despite the presence of Lady Lisle. Cressida had not felt it necessary to disclose anything of her own relationship with that woman, although she suspected it would not matter, as Aunt Delia had discovered her ladyship's unpleasant manners for herself. Unfortunately, as long as Lady Lisle remained a guest of Mrs Davies and a fixture in the community, even Cressida knew that to exclude her would be a gross social error.

They were not often in company together, and it seemed her ladyship would content herself with doling out menacing stares whenever Cressida happened to look upon her, for which Cressida suspected she ought to be grateful. It would never do for Aunt Delia to inquire into Lady Lisle's strange behaviour.

On this night, that woman seemed so preoccupied with ensuring her daughters danced with the most eligible men in attendance that she took no notice of Cressida, who could only hope that with the London season nearing full swing that lady would leave Frambury behind sooner rather than later.

'Miss Cressida?'

She started a little as Lord Windmere appeared at her side. He had only moments before been escorting Miss Heaston off the floor.

'May I have your next set?'

'Yes.' The word was automatic, and if she wished to continue dancing, she had no other choice than to agree, but when he took her hand in his and she became aware of the latent strength of his fingers as they wrapped around hers, she wished she had refused. She had often stood near him, but never *with* him. She had never laid a hand upon his arm, been able to feel the jump of a muscle as it moved under her touch. She had never been so aware of a body next to her own as she was his. The heat that surged through her had nothing to do with how many times she'd already stood up or how many people were packed into her aunt's ballroom.

The music began, and she focused on the steps in a paltry attempt to steady her breathing and direct her thoughts at something other than the man across from her. When he spun her halfway round, her arm for a moment held above their heads, she was sure he could hear the irregular drum of her heartbeat.

'You dance beautifully,' said Lord Windmere in hushed tones, his voice sweeping down her spine and pulsating through her limbs. She wondered if he could see the tiny shivers prickle the bare skin of her arms just above her gloves.

'Are you surprised to find such refinement in the country?'

'I am not surprised to find it in you.'

They parted for a step before coming together once more, his hand at her back, hers on his shoulder. Cressida was conscious of the hardness beneath her fingers, as if there weren't layers of fabric between them, conscious that the curve of his shoulder filled her palm and then some. She wanted to say something provoking, to remind herself how much she disliked this man who was so close to her she was made dizzy by the heady scents of bergamot and rosemary, sandalwood and fresh-shaven man. She wanted to distract herself from the acute awareness that all his attention was hers, that his eyes were asking her a question she didn't understand, that his full lips were just inches from her own, and from the unnerving curiosity to know how they'd feel against her own.

'Are you paying me a compliment or flirting with me, my lord?'

'Neither, Miss Cressida. Telling you how wondrous you look tonight, that's a compliment,' Lord Windmere replied as they completed another turn. He pulled her nearer, the hand at her back possessive and exerting more pressure than necessary. Then he dropped his head so his mouth was just a hair's breadth from her ear. 'Telling you how undone I am in your presence, that is flirting.'

His warm breath tickled the shell of her ear, and her mouth and throat felt dry and tight. When she dared to look up, his eyes had a disconcerting glow that had nothing to do with the candlelight flickering and reflecting within them. Her pulse, against all possibility, thumped with more rapidity, and she was certain he could discern as much in the vein in her neck as it pulsed and throbbed. He was holding her in a way entirely unfamiliar. The dance was not so different from any other, but his touch, how it felt to have his hand on her body, was. It brought to mind the day she'd met him, and the dangerous gleam in his eyes when their paths crossed as she went to retrieve her forgotten ribbon. Just as she did on that day, she recognised her desperate need to escape.

She finally worked to swallow but made no effort at a reply, and he, with exquisite tact, allowed them to finish their dance in charged silence.

'My lord.' Cressida eventually spoke as the dance ended and he led her from the floor. 'I believe I saw my sister moving in the direction of the retiring room and wish to ensure her well-being.'

'Of course.' He released her and bowed over her hand.

Cressida gave a small curtsey and, once they parted, moved past the retiring room and onto the library, determined to grab a moment of solace and settle the trembling of her limbs.

There were several candles burning, creating pockets of light in an otherwise dark room. It suited her, the darkness.

She sank into a plush chair upholstered in creamy red velvet halfway into the room, near an unlit fireplace, wishing she could hide there until the ball was over and knowing she couldn't.

She tore at the elbow-length gloves she wore and, once they were peeled off, wiped her sweating palms on the fine upholstery of the chair with a silent apology for the act. Her breath remained uneven, and she was unable to stay still, rising and sitting several times in quick succession as she tried to marshal her thoughts and chaotic feelings into some semblance of order when she heard the door open.

The library being in near total darkness mattered not. Even before he spoke, she traced the outline of his figure. After having a hand upon that muscular frame, she wouldn't soon forget it.

'What are you doing in here?' As she asked the question, she moved with determination to the door he'd just closed behind him. She was reaching for the handle, trying to ignore Lord Windmere, when the door flung open and several things happened at once: Cressida stumbled backwards; a pair of large, strong arms enveloped her; and Lady Lisle exclaimed, in a voice rife with feigned shock, 'My Lord Windmere! And Miss Cressida!'

14

_L_ucius had spent an inordinate amount of time these last weeks thinking of Miss Cressida Ambrose, or rather thinking of her, realising he was thinking of her, firmly resolving to put her from his mind, and repeating the entire process a short while later.

Their interaction at Dryce Hill had left him in foreign territory, and he was as unsettled as he was captivated, although he refused to acknowledge the latter of those two feelings. In the few meetings between them since, he'd been distantly polite, hardly a step above passably cordial at times, unwilling to spar with her as he had done until he was once more master of himself and his wayward thoughts. But then he came through the entrance at Blackbird Hall, up the stairs that would bring him to the ballroom, and of their own volition his eyes found her—and she took his breath away.

He asked her to dance, having convinced himself it was his duty as a guest to honour his hostess, but then her hand was on his arm, then _she_ was in his arms, and for the space of a waltz, Lucius gave himself leave to be someone else—someone who hadn't watched both parents fade away, someone who hadn't shouldered too much responsibility from too young an age, someone who could love and be loved without any understanding of what devastation could come from such a seemingly wonderful thing.

He considered himself relieved when she excused herself after their dance but found himself moving once more in her direction, unsure what exactly he meant to do or say, only having a vague sense that he wasn't quite ready to have done with her company.

Following her had been the only impulsive thing Lucius could ever recall doing, and when Lady Lisle appeared on the other side of the opened door to find Miss Cressida in his arms and the pair alone together in a dark room, he knew the deepest kind of regret.

It didn't go unnoticed by him that as the lady spoke, her head turned quickly from side to side. Whether there were in fact other people within hearing distance, or she was only hoping so, he couldn't determine. He also couldn't determine what kind of trap he'd been caught in when she stepped further into the room and closed the door behind her and her daughter, but that he was ensnared in something was certain.

'My, my, what a predicament we've found ourselves in.'

'I have not the luxury of understanding you, ma'am.' As the deep timbre of his voice filled the noiseless room, he felt a little tremor against his chest and realised his arms still held Miss Cressida. With movements as reluctant as they were determined, he released her and took up the space at her side.

Lady Lisle released a practised laugh. 'Oh, my lord, you've been caught in a passionate embrace with a local miss, which, naturally, no one would be surprised by, given your reputation.'

Lucius felt the muscle in his jaw tense, but said in an even, bored voice, 'Quite right. Nothing says passion like catching a stumbling woman.'

'You mistake the situation, ma'am.' There was a flinty quality in Cressida's reply Lucius had not previously heard.

'Do I?'

'Yes,' Lucius drawled, 'but the problem with the truth is that it's often rather boring.'

'Ah, we begin to understand one another.'

Lucius, ready for the woman to come to her point, asked without preamble, 'What's your play, Lady Lisle?'

'Really, my lord, you ought to call me cousin,' she replied with a sneer. 'There are two solutions to this little situation we've found ourselves in. First, I can sweep out of here and pretend nothing amiss has come to pass. I suspect I might appear a trifle overcome, but such astonishment cannot be easily borne by a female's natural delicacy of mind and it shreds our nerves, you understand. That being the case, my friends might be all compassion and concern, and while I wouldn't mean to, I may, in my confusion, confide in them the *shocking* scene I just witnessed. Your reputation, Lord Windmere, will make my version rather more believable, and yours, Miss Cressida, will be ruined before supper is announced.'

Lucius felt the anxiety rolling off Cressida, her whole body still and rigid next to his. Guilt, another feeling with which he was unfamiliar, very nearly bowled him over.

'Or?'

'Or you marry Anthea. She's a lovely girl, even you can admit, and she was raised to the role she'll occupy as your wife.'

He spared a look at his cousin, who was standing behind her mother and appeared equal parts surprised and mortified.

'You're willing to ruin an innocent young lady and her sisters just to see me married to your daughter?' he asked, with real curiosity.

'It's nothing she doesn't deserve,' Lady Lisle snapped, malice in her eyes, her air, the very being of her body. 'Frankly, I'd be equally pleased with either outcome.'

Lucius wouldn't betray the surprise he felt at such a claim. 'My grandfather was right to split from the family, and I believe he took all the goodness.'

As he spoke, he reached down to claim Cressida's hand and place it on his arm. He felt her tense and gave her hand a warning squeeze. 'Admittedly I'm no stranger to sneaking a tête-à-tête, as you know, and now I've a suspicion it was you who tried to give away the widow Avondale at the Colton masquerade. It is fortuitous for us, that in this case, the truth is likely to be of more interest than whatever tale you plan to carry forth from this room, which I don't doubt you will do and would have done regardless of whether I offered for Miss Heaston, which in any event I am unable to do.'

He watched the first inkling of doubt pass over the woman's countenance and savoured the moment. 'You know what's more likely to set tongues wagging than me being caught alone with a lady? My being engaged to one. I offered for Miss Cressida, and she accepted. Will you be the first to wish us joy?'

Lucius's pleasure in watching the colour drain from Lady Lisle's face was brought to an abrupt end when Cressida's hand squeezed his arm with an astonishing amount of strength and he gently put his other hand over hers, trying to subtly loosen her painful grip.

Her ladyship's eyes slimmed to angry, dubious slits. 'I don't believe you.'

'That matters not a whit to me. We can have nothing further to say to one another, ma'am. I'll only add that naturally I'll protect my betrothed and her reputation by any means necessary.' His charming smile did nothing to temper the venom in his voice. 'You'll excuse us while we resume our enjoyment of this evening.' Lucius led Cressida from the room and said in her ear, 'We should find your aunt and speak with her privately.'

He looked down at Cressida, who had said nothing for too long, and reached out his free hand to pinch her pale cheeks a little. When she started, he said, 'For someone who just secured quite the matrimonial prize, you look ghastly. It won't do. No one will believe I've finally deigned to get married if the lady has already lost her bloom.'

He teased as much to lift her spirits as his. He had done the unthinkable, the irrevocable, and the one thing he never wanted to do. All of London knew he didn't dally with innocents, and he suspected the thawing of the good people in Frambury and its surrounding villages meant they now knew it too, but none of that would matter when the whispers started. Cressida, however much good credit she had with her neighbours, wouldn't survive the scandal of being alone in a room with him, particularly not once Lady Lisle had her say in the story. That he'd never compromise a young lady wouldn't matter. What would matter is that they would tell themselves he had, just this once. If Cressida didn't understand as much, he did.

15

'*W*ell, you've really made a muddle of things. It's not how I would have had the situation unfold, but there's no denying the good that will come from it,' Aunt Delia said, after Lucius had laid out the whole of the scene in the library. The three of them had slipped to the study when dancing resumed after supper.

'You can't mean to make me go through with this!' Cressida exclaimed, pushing herself out of the chair from which she had originally collapsed. 'And you, my lord. How could you? How dare you?'

'I cannot make you do anything and wouldn't encourage you in a direction if you felt moral opposition to it, dearest. My advice to you, which is yours to do with as you please, is to allow the engagement to stand. We can announce it this evening, which should put Lady Lisle back in her box. She may kick up some dust regardless, but an engagement at least protects your reputation, and there is no need to marry in a hurry.' Aunt Delia paused, looking from one to the other. 'Right?'

'Aunt!'

Aunt Delia lifted one delicate shoulder in response. 'I will add, Cressida, that if you discover that you cannot abide a life tied to this gentleman, we can contrive to extricate you with as little damage as possible, but the truth is, our dear Lord Windmere has a reputation that precedes him.'

'I don't understand,' Cressida replied, resuming her seat and running a hand over her forehead in an attempt to rub away the headache forming.

'Engaged couples have more freedom.'

Cressida looked at her aunt in confusion and then to Lucius, whose cheeks were tinged by the barest hint of colour. It was such an odd sight, she almost smiled.

'Oh, dear,' sighed Aunt Delia. 'To put it bluntly, child, although no one would dare say so, it's unlikely anyone will believe you *haven't* been compromised—thoroughly—by the time you walk down the aisle.'

Cressida groaned and propped her elbows on the arms of the chair, allowing her to put pressure on her temples. Her eyes closed, and she worked her breath into something deep and rhythmic in an effort to keep herself from succumbing to her very first fit of the vapours. She felt someone come near her, and when she looked, she saw Lord Windmere kneeling in front of her. He took one of her hands, which she yanked right back. His head tilted in acknowledgement, and he made no further effort to possess any part of her.

'Miss Cressida—'

'There is nothing you can say which I have any interest in hearing.'

'Mrs Wright,' he said to her aunt, 'would you excuse us a moment?'

Cressida kept a wary eye on him as she heard the swish of

her aunt's dress and the click of the door as it closed. He moved a little away from her, and she took the opportunity to stand, straighten her skirts and her shoulders, and prepare for whatever battle she was about to enter.

'You are thinking only of your happiness and your reputation. What of mine?' he asked in his languid, vexatious way. 'I'm a lot of things, including an unapologetic lover of the feminine form. What I am *not* is a scoundrel. I've never in my life compromised or seduced an innocent, and I've no intention of letting such detestable rumours plague me, now or ever. Can you imagine what people would say? I'll tell you, my sweet. At best they would accuse me of being a blackguard, and at worst they would say Lucius Anselme has lost his touch and is now forced to pleasure ladies who have nothing else to compare it to.' He closed his little speech with a feigned shudder.

'So I am to marry you simply to spare your pride? I'm in raptures. I may even swoon. A rake with integrity. Have you another jest? The first was so reviving.' Cressida forced out a laugh that was supposed to sound mocking but only sounded a little hysterical. She didn't know what she was saying, only that she was perilously close to bursting into tears and the author of her misery was severely trying her patience.

His eyes darkened, and that unsettling gleam flickered. His index finger came up to drag across his bottom lip, revealing just a hint of straight white teeth, and as her breath stuttered in her chest, she wished her words unsaid.

'And this is what you think of me?'

He took a step towards her. She flinched but remained where she was, her body frozen and her heart hammering. He walked around her, his gaze roaming every inch of her body and his lazy, roguish half-smile indicating he liked what he saw. The direct attention tickled her already frayed nerves, and she began to feel a little lightheaded when he came to a standstill behind her.

Neither had their gloves on, and as his hands curved over her shoulders, his touch was so light she may have tricked herself into imagining it, if not for the warmth permeating the silky fabric of her dress. He ran his hands down the length of her bare arms; the movement was slow, caressing, and woke every follicle on her body.

His palms pressed against the back of her hands, and his elegant, skilled fingers pushed apart her own, making a space for his to settle. When his hands closed around hers, his long fingers stroking the sensitive flesh of her palms, her whole body trembled against the firmness of his. She felt the warmth of his breath on the nape of her neck and, with a sharp gasp, sucked in the first lungful of air she'd had in minutes when the tip of his nose nuzzled a previously unknown tender spot behind her earlobe.

She wanted to move, desperately needed to pry herself from his embrace before her compromise became a very real thing, but the sight of his hands covering her own, the feel of luxurious blue superfine grazing her skin, his scent on her and in her—when she managed to breathe, bergamot and something else unknown but decidedly *him* tickled her throat and poured through her. He caused her senses to unfurl. He introduced her to desire. And the sensations overwhelmed and confused her to such an extent, she wasn't sure she could find the door had she made the effort to do so.

Lord Windmere was still holding her left hand as he trailed his right hand back up her arm, grazed across the flesh of her breasts sitting above the neckline of her dress, and splayed his fingers against the exposed skin of her chest, his thumb and forefinger tracing along her collarbone.

Cressida was ready to cry out, to say whatever he wanted to hear that would put an end to the torment he was inflicting upon her, when he moved his hand up to gently grasp her throat, the tips of his fingers edging into her hair. She could hardly breathe, much less think or speak, and for one fleeting moment she almost wished his hand would tighten and end her embarrassment. Her whole body was vibrating—with fear, with yearning, and she knew he knew it.

His knuckles drew up to tease the soft flesh of her cheek and she felt herself lean into the small movement. Her body no longer felt like her own, no longer felt within her own control, and when he brought his lips to her jaw in a whisper of a kiss, Cressida moved with instinct but not thought, tipping her head to give him better access. He trailed one, two, three kisses, the last one feathering the very corner of her mouth, and she heard herself whimper from somewhere far away.

She waited for more, for his lips to press against hers, for her first taste of him, and was wondering what would happen if she just turned around in his embrace, when a cool blast of air hit her back, her body was freed, her fingers that had been curled around his, now empty.

She spun to face Lord Windmere, knowing her eyes were wide and wild, her chest heaving, her cheeks overcome with two unmistakable spots of red. He was entirely composed; the mouth which had just made her quiver was now set in a grim line, and there was a hardness in his blue-green eyes she couldn't make sense of in her haze.

'I could have had you here. I could have had you in the library.' His tone was savage, and Cressida felt all the air as it whooshed from her lungs. 'I could have had you bent over the counter of the bookshop had I wanted you that way. *My integrity is the only thing preserving your virtue.'*

She reeled as if he had physically struck her. Before she could mount a retort, challenge him for speaking to her in such an odiously disgusting way, he opened the door, ushered in her aunt, and closed it promptly behind him without looking back.

16

*L*ucius hadn't thought himself a petty man until he steered his mount in the direction of Red Fern Grange and contemplated other ways in which he could punish his betrothed for her words at the ball, which were as fresh in his mind as the way her body had reacted to his touch.

Her opinion of him was low—*that* he understood from her forthright way of speaking to him and the merest hint of tolerance expressed her captivating green eyes—but as a rule he remained untroubled by something as fickle as opinion. That she questioned his integrity and insulted his character so thoroughly, particularly after he had done the honourable thing to safeguard her future at the expense of his own—that was a transgression he felt less capable of forgiving.

There had been a moment that morning on Dryce Hill during which he'd thought they might be coming to understand one another, that they might set down their swords. He'd misread the situation, and the mistake rankled almost as much as her wilful misunderstanding of his character. It was in this sullen mood he made his way to his betrothed's home, a place heretofore only observed by him in passing. However, their engagement had been announced the night prior, many faces, he reflected, not expressing as much surprise as he would have expected, and so this morning he would pay a visit to her father, followed by a ride to London to see the marriage articles drawn up.

The idea of taking a wife made him wince. It was not so long ago he had been telling Aunt Bea he would do nothing of the sort. He did not want a wife; he did not want children. He did not want anything more he could lose. Even as he thought so, he felt the inevitability of the situation. He never allowed what he wanted to matter. He kicked Helios into a canter, wishing for the first time in years he could outrun his troubles.

Red Fern Grange, with its rows of tidy windows and vines weaving up the side, was the kind of quaint manor house that would charm any passer-by if the owner was willing to put in the minimum required to maintain it. Instead, it looked near abandoned—the exterior somewhere between shabby and dilapidated, the small garden set at its side the only thing worth looking at. Lucius was still trying to reconcile the spirited beauty to whom he was engaged with the neglected place she called home when a harassed-looking housekeeper cracked the front door open not quite wide enough to reveal her whole person.

'Lord Windmere for Mr Ambrose,' he said, without preamble.

The housekeeper looked over her shoulder at something Lucius couldn't see. 'I beg your pardon, my lord, but Mr Ambrose isn't at home to callers today.'

'Mrs—'

'Hutchins, sir.'

He offered a kind but close-lipped smile. 'Mrs Hutchins, one of my least favourite things is interfering with a capable housekeeper, which you seem to me to be, but I must insist on seeing Mr Ambrose.'

The ghost of a smile played upon the elderly housekeeper's lips before her face fell once more into a look of worried dismay. 'I'm really very sorry to refuse your lordship—'

Lucius missed the rest of what she said. A male voice, rising and falling in unmistakably angry tones, garnered all his attention.

'Mr Ambrose, I presume?'

Mrs Hutchins wouldn't meet his eyes and said in a beseeching tone, ''Tis nothing more than one of his freaks. He wears himself out quickly these days. If you'll come back some other time.' She was already shutting the door, but the tip of his boot prevented her from closing it upon him entirely. 'Please, m'lord,' she pleaded, 'interference only ever makes it worse.'

Lucius ignored her entreaties and pushed in easily, the slight housekeeper no match for his purposeful strength. Once inside, the warbled words of an incensed Mr Ambrose clarified. '*Disgraced. Disgusting. Doxy.*' By the time Lucius reached the door, which was not all the way closed, his own seething rage was exponentially greater than that of Mr Ambrose. He threw it open and barked one deafening word.

'Enough!'

Two stunned persons occupied the room. Lucius made the mistake of looking to Cressida first. She was standing tall and proud, her shoulders back, her chin up, but her countenance was pale and defeated, her eyes red and swollen, a continuous stream of tears rolled steadily and silently down her cheeks.

His fists clenched and his body coiled with restraint as he

imagined wrapping his hands around the lapels of Mr Ambrose's coat and slamming that man into the wall with such force the whole house would rattle. 'You will reconsider the language you use when speaking to my betrothed.'

'Betrothed, is it?' The man wheezed on the words, and Lucius watched as Mr Ambrose soothed his rough throat with a sip of something golden-brown in colour. Bile rose in Lucius's throat. 'The chit was speaking the truth then. I won't be sorry to see her go, but consider yourself warned: her mother only produced daughters and the one son she gave me never drew a breath. And this one—' Lucius watched with cautious interest as Mr Ambrose pinned his glassy eyes on his second child. 'Well.' The hand still holding the glass waved unsteadily back and forth, and whatever further insult her father had been poised to deliver went left unsaid. With an eye still on his daughter, he added, 'You're lucky any man is taking you, girl.'

Before Mr Ambrose could say more, Lucius turned to Cressida. 'I cannot like you remaining under this roof. Have a maid pack your things. You will go to your aunt's directly.' He watched her a moment. Her eyes appeared to him a little vacant, unseeing almost, but she nodded once in under-standing and Lucius turned back to Mr Ambrose. 'If you turn your temper on a new target, it won't be words I use to resolve the situation.'

Mr Ambrose sputtered, and his chest puffed in indignation, but he fell back in his chair, overtaxed and top-heavy.

Lucius ushered Cressida out of the room and urged her to her own. After she'd disappeared, he took to pacing the corridor until a door opened at the far end of it and Miss Ambrose's head peeked out. She said nothing, but concern was etched across her features. He moved in her direction, and when she stepped aside, allowing him to pass into the room, he saw that she was in company with her other two sisters, all three wan and fretful, worrying lengths of ribbon or pages of books. He had hardly the time to inform them of Cressida's change in residence before the lady herself reappeared, brushing off her sisters' expressions of concern. 'I'm fine. I'm fine, really, but I could do with some air.'

Lucius took that as his cue and offered her his arm. She placed one hand upon it with a hesitating look and with the other reached out to grasp her eldest sister's hand.

'You'll come to see me later?'

Only once the three remaining sisters agreed did Cressida allow him to turn her from the room and lead her from the house. They paused only long enough for him to leave word with Mrs Hutchins to expect his footmen, who would come to collect Cressida's things later that morning. The whole sequence of events struck him as rather unceremonious.

They walked in the general direction of Blackbird Hall, his horse following dutifully behind, with not a word exchanged between them for the first quarter of an hour.

'Cressida,' he began, his voice mild, concerned.

She shook her head. 'Please, don't, my lord.'

'Lucius,' he corrected. 'If you recall, I was present for some of the demonstration at least.'

'Stop.'

'You cannot expect me to believe you escaped that encounter unscathed. No one could.'

'Perhaps no one unaccustomed to that kind of behaviour.'

'Unaccustomed?' He stalled their progress. 'Do you mean to tell me your father regularly speaks to you in such a manner?' Given the language being used, Lucius had assumed that Mr Ambrose had misunderstood the situation being related, causing him to use language unfitting for a gentleman, particularly one addressing his own daughter. The fury that had finally burned itself out reignited.

'Please.' Her voice was hoarse, and the word came out scratched and harsh.

'Cressida.'

She yanked herself away from him. 'If you persist, I will walk straight into town and ruin your reputation and mine just so you have something else to occupy your mind. Is it not enough you forced me into this farce of an engagement? Now you'll force me to speak on something that can only give pain and embarrassment to me and—and—I know not what to you. Diversion? Triumph? Remorse for your hasty and ill-conceived act of gallantry? Why did you even come? You should not have done.'

Lucius held his hands up in acquiescence. Neither said a word until they'd ascended the steps of Blackbird Hall. When Cressida's aunt greeted them, surprise and curiosity playing across her face, he said, 'Miss Cressida can provide you the details.' Turning to Cressida, he added, 'I'm for London, but I'll call when I return at week's end.' He bowed over her hand, thinking better than to place a chaste kiss upon it, and retreated from the house, thinking only of getting as far from the tangle as possible.

17

*C*ressida kicked off her shoes and tucked up her stockinged feet as she settled into a window seat in the morning room at the back of the house. With a sigh, she watched her sisters' retreating forms as they made their way through the garden and towards the lane that would take them to the village. She had gone with Astrid once in the sennight since the ball and had the bad luck of running into Lady Lisle.

'What an unexpected pleasure.' The words had sliced their way out of the lady's mouth as Cressida and Astrid came face to face with her and her eldest daughter inside the mantua-maker, the four of them the only patrons in the shop. 'Naturally you would need some new dresses,' Lady Lisle added, letting her gaze fall to Cressida's midsection, the intimation clear to all parties.

'Naturally, as the future marchioness,' replied Astrid on behalf of her sister.

Her ladyship's eyes narrowed. 'Yes, how lucky for your sister. Will you think her lucky still when the marquess returns to romping around town, as he is bound to do once the lustre wears off his country bride?'

Anthea Heaston sucked in a sharp breath and uttered an aghast 'Mama,' which her mama paid no mind to.

'You're all concern, madam,' Cressida replied, with an evenness she was far from feeling. 'Let me put your mind at ease. With such resources at my disposable as Marchioness of Windmere, luck need not factor into my happiness.'

'I hope you never know the meaning of the word.'

Astrid stepped forward between the two. 'That's quite enough. We have all been very sorry for your loss, but it was no more Cressida's fault than the ground beneath your son. Come away, Cressie.'

'Hateful, hateful woman,' Cressida said, once the lady was away from the shop.

'Why do you let her words bother you when there's no truth in them?'

Cressida ran some fabric on a bolt between her fingers. 'There's no truth in Father's either, and still they sometimes prick.'

'Have you told Lord Windmere?'

'What is there to tell?'

Astrid laid a hand on her sister's arm. 'Our neighbours were satisfied putting a point on the viscount's time here, but that doesn't erase his existence or what he did to you.'

'At least she departs before the wedding, according to our aunt, so I am at liberty to think of her no more.'

The bell of a door chimed, and when both Ambrose sisters looked back from their closed conversation, they saw Miss Heaston approach alone.

'I beg your pardon, Miss Ambrose, Miss Cressida. I only wished to apologise for my mother's behaviour—not just today.' She glanced down at her gloved hands, which were tied up in one another. 'You deserve happiness, and I hope you find it in your upcoming union. Truly.' With that, Miss Heaston whisked herself back out of the shop, leaving the Misses Ambrose wide-eyed and speechless.

That was the second worst day since her engagement, the first being the morning after, which began with Cressida in an apprehensive mood. Knowing her father would somehow learn about the engagement, she thought it best to reveal the news herself and get whatever unpleasantness was sure to be the result done with.

His outpouring of vitriol surprised even her, and from that moment, her mood had undergone so many alterations it was impossible to keep track: shock, anger, denial, disappointment, frustration, and, at being ordered to remove from her home, indignation, which prevented her from framing that piece of business as it deserved. and rather had her categorising it as another example of Lord Windmere's high-handedness.

Her sisters had come to Blackbird Hall later that same day, but whatever dour expression was upon her face prevented them from asking questions or pushing for explanation. Of course, in the days following, some account was required, and although she took Astrid into her confidence, pouring out the whole miserable tale and her wretched feelings along with it, she permitted her younger sisters to think there was nothing the least irregular in the match, aside from the very great disparity in rank, and allowed them their hopeful faces and excited exclamations, for having a marchioness as a sister surely meant a London season.

Cressida was not so insensible as to look at their worn dresses and walking boots and not think on how much she might be able to do for them. Aunt Delia couldn't be expected to provide for all of them indefinitely, after all. If only it had been someone else, someone not connected to a family she loathed, some gentleman she could perhaps at least like, and who did not exasperate her beyond reason.

In moments she was feeling petty and spiteful, she'd think it his just deserts that he'd tied himself to a woman of questionable birth. The rest of the time, she knew what a mean trick it was to keep that fact from him. It was unlikely her father would ever reveal the truth, but it wasn't impossible, and that trace of possibility always brought her up short. It was wrong to marry Lord Windmere without him knowing, but the idea of confiding in him made her stomach clench. This was the thought upon which she was still dwelling when masculine, purposeful steps sounded in the hall.

She looked up from the window seat in time to see Lord Windmere come to a stop in the doorway. His dark hair was a little unruly, his bright eyes unfocused but somehow still intent on her. After the ball, it was impossible for Cressida to unsee him or to prevent herself from imagining what his body looked like under his elegant, tailored clothes, each piece designed to display his perfect proportions, the power beneath the expensive fabric. She flushed under his gaze, and the rhythm of her traitorous heart increased.

'Perhaps your aunt is available to join us?'

'I thought engaged couples were given more latitude,' she answered dryly.

The quip earned her a lopsided grin. He produced a thick sheaf of papers. 'Marriage articles would typically be reviewed by your father.'

'Oh.' It was a stupid response. She knew Lord Windmere would have nothing further to do with that man, and neither would she.

'I don't doubt your abilities, but your aunt, at the very least, is likely to have a solicitor who can review these on your behalf. In the meantime, I'd like for you to review them yourself and let me know if there is anything you're dissatisfied with.'

He came over to where she was still perched in the window seat and sat next to her, his thigh only an inch from her own, and resting the papers on top of his legs, briefly explained that the most significant figures would naturally be her pin money and the provisions made for her should she outlive him.

Cressida stared at the profile of her betrothed. His voice was even, but she noted his shoulders held some tension; the muscle in his jaw flexed several times, suggesting irritation or perhaps impatience. He tapped his index finger on the page, and she remembered that finger tracing the upper swell of her breast, trailing along her collarbone. Heat flooded her from the inside out, and she pressed the back of her hand to her forehead as if the feeble gesture could quell the frenzy stirring inside her.

'Are you all right, Cressida? Ought I to ring for your aunt?'

Lord Windmere was looking at her, but she kept her head down, sure he could see the splotches of red on her neck and cheeks nonetheless. She opened her mouth a little and tried to fill her lungs. 'Yes.' The word sounded like it had been peeled from her throat. 'Quite.'

He watched her a moment longer before drawing her focus to where his finger rested on the paper, just below an exorbitant figure.

'My lord!' She recoiled as if the paper could burn her. 'I cannot agree to these terms.'

He looked at her with a furrowed brow. 'I'll own to

knowing a little something of women's fashions. I had thought this ample pin money, but I'll defer to your expertise.'

'You misunderstand. This is too much.' She would bring nothing to a marriage she did not want. To take anything from him was anathema to her, but taking so much was not to be borne.

'You sell yourself short, pet,' he replied, with a flash of an impish smile. 'There's no price I wouldn't pay for security from matchmaking mamas.'

It was meant as a jest, she knew, and yet she found herself replying with more rancour than intended. 'Of course, you are only thinking of yourself.'

One thick, straight brow rose. 'You will add selfish to my list of crimes? I had not thought you room for more.'

'Do you have a better way of describing your behaviour? Because such a label seems fitting when one is forced into marriage by another to spare *his* reputation.'

'It's not too late for you to make your escape.'

A funny little sound of disagreement burst forth from her mouth. 'If you recall, some months ago I told you I had no ambition to marry. Perhaps you heard that as some maidenly piece of folly, but I was genuine in my claims, and what now? A life I didn't want thrust upon me without thought or care for what I may feel, what I may want.'

'You harp on as if you're alone in not getting what you want. I recall, during that same conversation, expressing with perfect truth and clarity my own desire to remain a bachelor.'

'And yet—'

He cut her off. 'And yet I put my desire aside to prevent the complete ruination of your family.'

'Without consulting me!' She knew how ridiculous she

sounded, but she could not find it within her to agree with him, no matter how correct he was in his point.

'How right you are. Perhaps I should have, under the baleful stare of Lady Lisle, asked which was preferable to you. By the by, she made a rather odd comment about you, did she not?'

Cressida's heart gave one hard thud in her chest, but she went on as if he had not asked the question at all. 'So, this'— she gestured vaguely at the papers on his lap—'is payment for what exactly? Being your brood mare until there's an heir?' The words felt coarse and vile in her mouth as she said them. She had jumped from her seat to stand in front of him and was given the rare opportunity to look down into his eyes. Cressida expected to see mockery, smugness maybe, but instead she thought he looked a little wounded, but only for a second, before derision hardened his features.

'If I expected your body in return for my wealth, that would make you an altogether different kind of woman than the one I thought you to be.'

Cressida's wrath swelled quickly and completely, and although her mouth gaped in shock, she had not yet recovered from the injury enough to make a reply.

'I've no need for a *brood mare*—language unbecoming of any gentle female, particularly one soon to be elevated to great heights, so let us retire that word from your lexicon. More to the point, I've no interest in forcing my attentions upon an unwilling recipient and, frankly, no need. I've no affinity for the title. It would be rather poetic, in fact, if a bastard inherited it when I'm gone, so you need not be overly concerned to that end. You may keep to your own rooms and take a lover if it pleases you to do so.'

'No doubt that's what you intend to do yourself.'

He made no answer but rose and placed the sheaf of papers on the seat he'd just vacated. 'I'll leave you with these and bid you good day, ma'am.'

When he had quit the room, from real weakness of mind and body, Cressida crumpled to the floor, where she remained until her aunt entered some three-quarters of an hour later.

'Oh, child. What's this nonsense?' Aunt Delia rang for tea first before taking Cressida by the elbow and leading her to a divan on one side of the room, situated near a charming painted table.

Cressida offered a rambling, incoherent explanation, unable or rather too uncomfortable to reveal the whole of the exchange.

'To break the engagement will not be without some discomfort, and very likely, doing such would necessitate your removal from this neighbourhood to one farther flung. I'd been looking forward to beginning anew in London, having a life of my own for the first time, but, well, needs must.' Aunt Delia squeezed Cressida's hand.

Guilt penetrated Cressida's disorderly thoughts. Her aunt had blown in like a summer storm, quick and furious, and taken control of the Ambrose sisters' situation without so much as a hair escaping a pin. She made it all seem easy and natural, and not once had Cressida considered what the lady would be doing were she not here with them. Cressida had accused Lord Windmere of selfishness, and yet it was she who thought only of herself.

'Did your mama share much with you about how I met my husband?'

'Only that you were in love with a man your family thought beneath you to marry, and Father exposed your plans to elope.'

'That's right, but it is only part of the story. I was quite young, hardly eighteen, and my parents told me I'd make my curtsey to the queen the following spring. It seemed impossible that I should, when I felt myself very much in love with Mr Harding, the curate. He'd taken the post the year prior, and from the moment I saw him, I felt surely he must be the man for me. He was a stunning creature, with more countenance than any man of the cloth had a right to, in addition to being full of warmth and kindness. I was too young then, too naïve to understand the difference between being treated a certain way because of *what* I was rather than *who* I was.

'At the very least, a clergyman willing to elope should have enlightened me. Mr Harding wasn't a bad man, and he was very good at the post he occupied, but until he took orders and moved to our little hamlet, he had lived a life with finer things than his occupation alone could provide and had yet to accustom himself to his new way of living. If you were to ask me whether I believed him to have real regard for me, I would say "yes" then and now. My dowry was not my only asset, but it was undoubtedly the one that interested him most.'

By now, Cressida had forgotten the worst part of her own morning and was entirely engrossed in her aunt's tale, hardly breathing for fear the slightest sound might bring the story to an abrupt halt.

'My brother, in whom, in my foolish desperation, I confided—for he had never been a kind or helpful soul— revealed my plan to elope to my father and was rewarded for it. The greater reward, however, went to Mr Harding. My father, for all his blustering and hard manners, would have done what he could to smooth over the scandal had I eloped. He was a man of position, and reputation was everything to him, you understand. Knowing of the plan wasn't enough. He went directly to Mr Harding and offered the man six thousand pounds. Mr Harding accepted it without quibble or consideration; the gentleman himself owned to that fact. I was devastated, and all hope seemed lost, so I accepted my father's ultimatum and wed Mr Wright a short while later.

'He was eight years older than myself and good enough to let me grieve the loss of innocence that comes from having one's eyes opened to the ugly truths that exist in the world. It was this first act of kindness that endeared him to me. We split our time between London and his family estate for some years before the desire to go abroad overcame us both, and we set off for India. Edmund and I did not begin in love with one another, but we discovered common interests and cultivated others together. Long before he departed this earth, he held my heart, and when he did go, it broke.' Aunt Delia dabbed the corner of her eye with a handkerchief. 'Things go on in unlooked for, unanticipated ways all the time. We hurt, we learn, we go on, and that is life. Love can grow from unexpected sources, but it must be given the chance.'

Aunt Delia rose, kissed the top of Cressida's head, and left that young lady contemplating the intricate pattern of vines and flowers and tigers on the rug beneath her feet.

18

*L*ucius had remained in London longer than necessary; in truth he could have written of his impending marriage to Hanks and spared himself the travel entirely if not for his desire to put physical distance between his person and his betrothed.

He'd kept the knocker off the door, avoided his clubs, and saw no one aside from his solicitor and Lord and Lady Dane, whom he took into his confidence—a decision he immediately regretted when it was met with Lady Dane's cheerful effusions and a penetrating stare from Lord Dane that hinted he understood more than perhaps even Lucius himself.

By the time he was once more on the road to Frambury, he owned himself anxious to see Cressida's lovely face and felt he had discovered some little peace with his situation. Lucius was no stranger to doing hard things, and marriage, he was sure, would number among those, but he'd consoled himself with the idea that if he must take a wife, there were far worse candidates than Cressida Ambrose, who was as spiky as she was lovely.

The careful weave of his rationale had come undone nearly as soon as he entered the door of Blackbird Hall, marriage articles in hand. His jest and generosity had twisted into selfishness, and as she hurled one insult at him and then another, he'd capitulated under the weight of his own ire. It was undignified, ungentlemanly, and his being ashamed of himself and his behaviour even in the moment hadn't been enough to prevent him leaving her standing there, mouth agape, words he hadn't meant lingering in the air.

He entered his own home with an ominous expression upon his face, and when his aunt pounced from the doorway of the frontmost salon, a room hardly used and where she'd surely been lying in wait, his countenance darkened further still.

'Went well with your future marchioness, then? Were you a shocking penny-pinch with her pin money?'

His aunt was ribbing him. She'd met Cressida several times since arriving at Tamarix Hall, among those occasions the monthly card party at the Harland residence and tea with Mrs Peregrine, where all the Ambrose sisters were present. She'd declared them all unexceptional young ladies. Her saying so had made him immediately suspicious. While his aunt was not lacking in kindness, she kept her nose a little in the air and was considered captious by those who knew her best.

When he'd come into the breakfast parlour the morning after the ball, from which she had abstained on account of a lingering cold, and announced without preamble his engagement to the second eldest unexceptional Ambrose daughter, his aunt had looked up, surveyed him without betraying surprise or judgement, and stated in a cordial way, 'I wish you joy,' before turning back to the letter in her hand. Her mild reaction had been disconcerting.

'You'll forgive me, ma'am, for desiring a moment of solitude,' he said presently, and with stinging impatience, as he turned on his heel.

'Lucius Theodore Elias Anselme.' She punctuated each of his names, halting him mid-stride. 'Do you intend to cast off Miss Cressida?'

'No,' he responded in a colourless voice.

'And she?'

There was a considerable pause before he answered. 'To the best of my knowledge, no.'

'A lifetime is a long time to indulge in a fit of the sullens.'

Lucius compressed his lips to withhold the peevish retort that sprang to mind and silently chided himself for his uncharacteristic petulance.

'Whatever is plaguing you, sort it out. You've no choice now, and neither does she.' Aunt Bea brushed past him, the tip of her walking stick landing squarely on the top of his boot as she did so

That night was a restless one for Lucius, during which his mind was primarily occupied in berating him for being so foolish as to fight against an inevitable outcome. He knew better; he had known better for almost two decades. From a young age he'd developed an impenetrable armour, the kind that made him impervious to flattery, to threats, to the sometimes true and sometimes false words spread across the scandal sheets. Words had never much mattered to him—it was often much easier to say something than to do something. But when Cressida spoke, her words took up residence within him. Their ability to do so, when he allowed his mind to consider the matter, was equal parts extraordinary and unwelcome.

On the following day, not long before the dinner hour, the

door to his personal sitting room, a sad, drab space that typically went unused except for moments he wished to remain undisturbed, was pushed open and Lucius sighed, thinking himself caught out by his aunt and soon to be subjected to another lecture he felt incapable of enduring. He was, therefore, entirely unprepared to set eyes upon Alexander's face.

'What the deuce are you doing here?' Lucius set the book of poetry he'd been reading down and reached out a hand to greet his brother.

'Mrs Yates told me where to find you and to keep your location to myself,' Alexander said with a knowing smile.

'Not this room, you young fool. What are you doing at Tamarix?' Lucius moved to close the door and gestured for his brother to take a seat before going to the understocked sideboard. 'I've only this awful sherry in here, although Mrs Yates will perhaps contrive to send up something more palatable now that she's aware of your presence.'

Alexander, taking a sip from the offered glass, grimaced. 'To answer your question, when one's brother says he's to be married, one presents himself.' After a pause, he added with a note of inquiry. 'Miss Cressida?'

There was little point in keeping something from Alexander, so Lucius unfolded the whole of the tale, only vaguely alluding to how he found himself also in the library.

'Well,' Alexander began, his face upturned in thought, 'I don't find it at all surprising.'

'The only surprising element is that Lady Lisle had not hatched a better scheme to ensnare me for her own daughter. It's odd, though, when one considers it. I've a hunch it wasn't at all planned, but more the opportunity of the moment, although I cannot puzzle out why.'

Alexander levelled an unflinching stare at his brother. 'That is not what I was referring to, Luci.'

Lucius picked up the decanter a silent and inconspicuous footman had just delivered and poured two fingers for his brother and himself. His attention, all on the task at hand, precluded him from seeing his brother's curious expression while he put forth the question, 'Alexander, do you think I'm a selfish being?'

'I think you're used to getting your own way—a very natural result of your upbringing.'

'That sounds very much like a yes.'

'What's brought this about? You've never been concerned with other people's opinions before, especially not mine.' Alexander was teasing again, but there was a kernel of truth tucked in his words.

'I thought only of myself when I brought about this engagement.'

Alexander looked on as Lucius spun the half-full glass of brandy around in the palm of his hand. 'That doesn't sound like you, Luci.'

'You just said—'

'I said you're used to getting your own way because you are. You are also the most accommodating, considerate person I know when you want to be.'

'I was neither of those things where Miss Cressida is concerned.'

'You feel you ought to have called Lady Lisle's bluff? Ignored her ultimatum and strode from the room as if nothing happened?'

'The cat wasn't bluffing. Her hostility towards Cressida was unnerving. There is no doubt she would have swept from the room and told everyone she passed what she saw, likely with a few new details—perhaps Cressida's dress torn, or my cravat undone. I'd have to marry her anyway, then, except everyone would think I was only doing it because I had already ruined her.'

'This was your way of protecting her reputation or yours? I begin to understand you.'

Lucius couldn't help smiling. No one knew him as well as his younger brother.

'It seems to me there was nothing else to be done, no other way for you to act in that moment. Miss Cressida is both intelligent and pleasant to look at. It would be surprising if she turns out to be anything other than a perfectly charming wife, even if her connections and dowry are not what you could command as a marquess, but those things don't weigh with you in the least, I know.'

Lucius kept his head down and his eyes averted from his brother's. 'She's as good as any other—better, even, since she has no interest in me,' he added, with a laugh that was a little too tight. 'She can use her position to sponsor her sisters and help them find good matches, I'll no longer be hunted, and we can continue on almost as if nothing had changed for either of us.' Alexander was watching him, Lucius could feel it, but he took a sudden interest in his nails, which prevented him from looking anywhere else.

Alexander said nothing but made a little humming sound tinged with disbelief.

Recognising an end to his peace, Lucius suggested a game of billiards and was already at the door before his brother could reply.

19

'There are worse men to have as your betrothed, you must admit,' Sophia said, jabbing a needle through her sampler. Cressida sat in the sunny parlour of the parsonage, a trifle irritated that the weather was misaligned with her mood.

'I wish you would open yourself a little to him. He's a good man, when all things are weighed.'

'I don't care for this topic. Choose another.'

'It matters to me. You are the closest thing I have to a sister, and if you continue at your current pace, you and he will be living separate lives and hardly able to look at one another across the table before your maid has unpacked your trousseau.'

Cressida didn't know how to tell her nearest friend that that was exactly what her intended wanted, so instead she said, 'What did you think of the gown Miss Samon wore to the ball? The lace was lovely.'

'Cressie, you will not talk me out of this. If you run to the trees, I will run after you. If you lock yourself in your room, I'll get the keys from the housekeeper.' Sophia's face was set with concern, and Cressida realised there was no escaping the topic at hand.

'I've no interest in marriage, in being at the mercy of another man, or in attempting to reform a rake, particularly one who has no interest in being reformed.'

'Who said anything about reforming the man? Men keep lovers, it's what they do.' Only after she'd said so did Sophia cast a look about to ensure they were well and truly alone. 'Did you expect him to cast off who he is the minute he proposed?'

He hadn't proposed, Cressida realised. Lord Windmere had made a statement, and the thing was done.

'And I know you think him very handsome.'

'I do not.'

'You do, and you may as well admit it.'

'Fine. He's not horrible to look at—maybe even everything a man ought to be, if he possibly can, in that sense.' Cressida could picture him then standing before her at the bookshop, a handsome stranger to whom no other gentleman could compare. She could see his rich tobacco-brown hair, the kind of hair that when he pushed his hand through it, sprang right back to life. She thought of his face, his square jaw and resolute chin, the full lips that had touched the bare skin of her cheek. Her breath grew shallow, and she wished for a fan. She kept her face averted to hide her blush.

'What else?'

'Nothing.'

Sophia's sigh was the vocal equivalent of rolling her eyes. 'He's kind.'

'Perhaps he's scared the bucolic village folk will take a torch to Tamarix.'

'You cannot find fault in his care of his staff and tenants.'

'He's doing just what he ought.'

'He's worlds better than the previous marquess, which shows what a responsible, considerate estate owner he is—perhaps the kind of husband he could be, with a little time.'

Cressida counted to ten in her head so she wouldn't snap at her friend. Sophia was doing what she thought was helpful, but Cressida wanted to scream at her to stop, to tell her this marriage would never be anything other than a sham.

'What of his kindness to you? Surely the Marchioness of Windmere will have such means of procuring her health and happiness at her disposal as to make all the rest insignificant.'

All the rest being love, fidelity, children—things Cressida hadn't known she wanted until she couldn't have them. The words echoed those Cressida had said herself; they were disingenuous then and painful to think on now. She was grateful when Mrs Harland returned home, putting an end to their private tête-à-tête.

Having no desire to enter marriage and give control of her person to another, Cressida should have felt relief when her betrothed claimed, in cutting accents, that he had no interest in asserting his marital rights. Instead, she was mortified and felt the insult down to her very core. Her friend was well-meaning, but their discussion had only further unsettled her. And her aunt's counsel, while worthy of examination, had been given too close to the injury to act as a balm. Rather than imagine herself content at some not-so-far-away point in the future, Cressida was plagued by ideas of an uncomfortable life with a disagreeable man, not so different from the life she currently led. It was in this bleak state of mind she greeted Lord Windmere as he entered the music room at Blackbird

Hall several days later to find her haphazardly plinking keys on the pianoforte.

'Will you ever call me Lucius? I wish you would,' he said with uncharacteristic openness. 'Are you well?'

'Fine. And you?'

'Quite well. Thank you. Your sisters?'

'Also well.'

They stared at each other in silence, letting time tick by until the decorative mahogany and brass clock on the mantel struck the hour and its musical bells chimed.

'I thought perhaps you'd like to walk with me today. The weather is particularly fine.'

Cressida eyed his lordship with open suspicion. He seemed amiable, engaging, not at all the man whose scathing words had brought her to her knees and ushered in several sleepless nights. She consented to his invitation and excused herself to collect her outdoor things.

Awkwardness settled between them as they fell into step on the lane, and she was debating whether she felt antagonistic, tired, hopeless, or something else altogether when he spoke.

'Is something on your mind?'

'I'm marrying a man I neither know nor like—of course something is on my mind.' She withheld a frustrated sigh and followed her outburst with an apology. Aside from no longer understanding how she felt about this man, he was, it seemed, entirely sincere in his inquiry and not seeking to cross swords.

Far from being offended, the lilt of her companion's mouth suggested he found some measure of amusement in her tetchiness, which only further bewildered her.

'I prefer antipathy to indifference.'

She tilted her chin up, but neither looked at him nor made a reply.

'There was a time I thought you were coming to understand me quite well,' he revealed in a low, quiet voice.

Cressida finally looked over at him then. He was staring at some point unseen by her. The edges of his mouth had turned down in a suggestion of a frown. The abrupt confession confused her in its content more than its delivery and, unsure how to respond, she said, 'Tell me about your life before arriving at Tamarix.'

The confiding air with which he had made his previous statement left him. 'That's a tall order when one has more than thirty years at one's back,' he replied with that lazy half-smile.

Cressida paused, turned, and considered the man at her side with unabashed interest, feeling for a moment as if she'd caught fire when she recalled what it felt like to have that chest pressed to her back, that mouth on her jaw, those hands wrapped around her own.

His mouth quirked and she wondered if he'd noticed the faint blush that rose in her cheeks. 'Well?'

With an absurd and discordant jolt of humour, Cressida admitted to him she had not the slightest idea how old he might be, although she was certain he couldn't be *that* old. The resulting laugh, a full, gravelly sound she had never heard, startled her, making Lord Windmere's shoulders shake with mirth.

'I am two-and-thirty.'

Her fair eyebrows lifted. 'Then tell me about your two-and-thirty years before arriving at Tamarix. You may start with the most recent, if you'd like.' Spoken as a demand, her application was softened by a small smile, which faltered a little when she saw him looking at her in the oddest way. It sent a strange sensation through her, and she became suddenly aware that they were still standing very near to one another—nearer, Cressida thought, than when they'd first stopped. Who had closed the distance, she couldn't be sure. She turned again, forcing him to resume their walk.

'I had another estate, Branford Park, inherited from my father, about a half-day's ride from here. It belongs to Alexander now.'

'You gave it to him?' Cressida tried and failed to keep the wonder from her voice.

'Branford is beautiful inside and out. My mother had wonderful taste, and my father let her do as she pleased with the house and grounds. It has been a good home to me, but now that I have the pile here, along with several others, I've not the time to enjoy it as it deserves. Alexander will make an excellent custodian, and as a man of property he will be able to marry where he chooses.' The words were truthful and said without bitterness of spirit, but the implication, real or imagined, was like a splinter under Cressida's nail.

'Unlike you.'

'There are many things we only frame as choices to make ourselves feel better. It's your turn. Tell me about your life before I arrived.'

'There's very little to say.'

'I disagree. I haven't pressed, but as your intended, I think I've a right to know a little something about your life before I became a part of it. Tell me of your mama.'

She folded her lips and fidgeted with her skirts. 'My mother was much too good for this world, which is probably why she's no longer part of it.'

After a silence extending beyond a minute, Lord Windmere spoke, accents of stony hauteur underpinning his words. 'Is that all the reply to which you feel me entitled as your future husband?'

'Better words I could not have chosen.' Cressida felt herself beginning to unravel, conscious that she was making an effort to cause a quarrel, despite not having the least desire to do so. It was as if things had been too peaceable between them for too long, that the glimpse she'd been given into one potential future seemed to her so implausible, her mind had no choice but to reject it.

As if exercise alone could put a period to this encounter, she increased her pace, thinking herself several steps ahead of Lord Windmere until a large hand wrapped around her arm, bringing her to a halt and compelling her to turn to face the man. He appeared to be struggling for composure, his normally full lips pressed into a hard, firm line, his eyes growing darker with every moment.

She shook him off. 'You availed yourself of my hand, bestowed upon me a type of kindness I neither desired nor asked for, and while as a woman I may have decidedly few options except to submit to your whims and wishes, I am under no obligation to expose the interiority of my mind to you. You can have no claim upon my thoughts.'

He started, coloured a very little, and when he replied, it was without a trace of his usual composure. 'No, I have no claim on your thoughts, and yet how often you've made me privy to those most unjust and unkind. You mistake me completely if you think my desire is to lay claim to a mind with such insufficient regard for civility or one mired in the kind of general inflexibility that prevents it from examining the impetus for those thoughts which it produces. My desire, ma'am, was an honest conversation with the woman to whom I am bound, free from the hostility, the antagonism, the very

173

prejudice that has, from the beginning, set you against me. I see now the mistake I made in considering you capable of such a burden and will refrain in future from making demands on your probity, your civility, and your candour.'

Cressida flushed with shame, which, when expressed, took the form of righteous anger. She hardly waited for his mouth to snap closed before she came about with a rebuttal.

'Candour? Probity?' Without having been sure what she would say once she started, as those two words dropped into the fraught space between them, the rest became clear. 'Very well. My father treats me the way he does because he believes me another man's child. My mother was assaulted, and I arrived some nine months later.'

Lord Windmere's astonishment was obvious. His whole body had gone frightfully still, his mouth fell open, his eyes went as wide as a child's at Christmastime.

'You see, sir, I am quite capable of the kind of reply you so desired, only you may find yourself less appreciative of the response once you have it.' She had stunned him into silence, as she knew the disclosure must, but her satisfaction withered as she began to think on the full implications of what she'd just done.

'You may give notice for our broken engagement however you see fit, only I ask for your discretion, as my dubious beginning remains a well-kept secret, even from those closest to me. If it was just myself, I'd care not, but for my sisters...' In one moment, she was exhilarated, the next she was overcome by the folly of her actions. She abhorred the idea of marriage because of the power it gave a man, but what had she just done if not that very thing, and without any of the protections bestowed upon a married woman? She gave Lord Windmere the power to ruin her and her sisters, to compel her into doing whatever she must to protect the secret she'd so closely guarded and so easily gave away in a fit of pique.

How long they remained standing there in their respective silences, Cressida could only guess at. On the verge of being released from the engagement, her thoughts began to swoop and dart and dip in such erratic and unexpected directions that she jumped when he asked in a composed, almost hesitant way, 'Is that what you want?'

Caught in the sudden, meaningful turn of her mind, she struggled to make sense of what he was asking and responded only with a confused bobble of her head and a furrowed brow.

He clarified. 'For me to send notice that our betrothal has come to an end?'

'I—I presumed that the natural conclusion to my admission.' She swallowed the sudden sense of panic that began to rise within and fought against her lungs, which seemed to be working harder and faster to take in air.

'Cressida?'

He was no more than an arm's length from her, closer even, and she considered for a moment what would happen if she just reached out into the space between them.

'Cressida.' Lord Windmere said her name again, softly, gently even. 'Is that what you want? You have only to say so.'

Contrary to what he'd said earlier, the day was not particularly fine. Greyish-white clouds obscured most of the sky overhead, the wind kicked up at odd intervals, and yet imperceptible beads of sweat prickled at her hairline and between her shoulder blades.

'No.' The word, when it came out, was little more than a whisper, but as she said it, it felt much more like a prayer.

20

_I_ n the days following his betrothed's stunning admission, Lucius saw her in company three times: once at the Hobbses', where their conversation was limited to such safe subjects as the weather and the origins of an interesting vase on an end table; once at an assembly where he partnered her twice but left early on account of his aunt; and once at his own home, to which Cressida and her aunt had been invited to dine.

'Perhaps after the meal you'll allow me to conduct you on a short tour of the primary rooms. You may make note of anything you wish to change,' Lucius said, as the gathered company, which included his aunt and brother, tucked into the soup.

'Everything, if the young lady has any taste,' his aunt said between spoonfuls.

Cressida was quick to pick up this thread. 'What if I'd like to repaper the house, in its entirety?'

'You may do as you like.'

'And replace all the old, uncomfortable furniture?'

'Certainly.'

'And build a new wing specifically for my own use?'

The corner of his lip twitched, but he maintained an air of seriousness as he said, 'Do me the honour of seeing the wings I have available for you at present. If none are to your liking, or you find they're lacking the distance between us you'd prefer, I'll construct you one of your very own.'

The smile she shared then, genuine, guileless, felt as if it was for only him, and indeed he'd managed to forget about the three others sitting at the table, looking between themselves with varying degrees of amusement.

Lucius had, at first, been unsure how to proceed after Cressida's confession, debating with himself late into the night how best to address what she'd said. But when he saw her at the Hobbses', and for the first time noticed uncertainty in her manner, he realised what was most important was putting her at ease. He had no wish for her to labour under the misapprehension that he may at any moment change his mind or to feel that the circumstances under which she'd arrived in this world somehow made any difference to him in regard to their future together.

The best course forward, he'd decided, was simply to do nothing—to go on as if nothing had changed, because for him, at least, it hadn't. The tension in her, and in their interactions, began to uncoil, and that, for him at least, was ample reward.

True to his word, Lucius took her through the main rooms of the house after dessert, but instead of guiding her back to the drawing room to join the rest of the small party, he steered them out to the veranda. The air was warm, hinting summer was no so far at hand, and alive with crickets beginning their night song as dusk settled around them.

Together they went down the further set of stairs and,

without knowing where exactly he was leading her, Lucius turned left and took them around the side of the house, where there existed a small garden, well-kept but with an air of wildness about it.

'Are those strawberries?' Cressida asked, releasing his arm and walking towards a stack of planter boxes with greenery cascading down and little pops of red beginning to peek through.

'The old lord had an affinity for them, or so I've been told by the head gardener. My mother did as well. There's a whole field of them at Branford.' He walked up alongside her. She was cradling a berry on her slender fingertips, examining its colour and size and shape.

'Have you ever seen a berry more perfect?'

He wasn't looking at the strawberry when he answered. 'No. It's a little early in the season yet, and most of these aren't ready for picking, but that one...' He let his words trail off and reached out to pluck the ripe strawberry from the stem on which it hung. She was watching his movements with interest, and after holding her gaze for a moment, his eyes drifted to her lips, which were parted ever so slightly.

Lucius, with the kind of slow movement typical in a dream, swept her bottom lip with the ripe red tip of the fruit before pausing to let it rest in the middle. Cressida sunk her teeth into its juicy flesh, her eyes never leaving his. He bit the remainder and let the delicate sweetness fill his mouth. A taste of juice ran down his thumb, but rather than reaching for his handkerchief, he caressed her lower lip once more and watched as her tongue instinctively brushed along the same course.

Somewhere at a distance church bells chimed the hour. Nearby a goldfinch trilled. Closer still Lucius could hear the thump of his own heart as it pounded in his chest. He ignored it all and took Cressida's face between his hands. Her eyes drifted closed, and there was nothing else then except for him and her and that moment.

Lucius dipped his head, paused for a second to run his eyes over her exquisite face, and with delicate, unhurried care, touched his lips to hers. They were supple and yielding against his own when his tongue sought permission to deepen the kiss. She responded with a soft whimper of pleasure, and he growled into her mouth as he pulled her body flush against his. He could feel the fullness of her breasts against his chest as he guided her arms up around his neck. She tugged on a curled lock of his hair and dipped her fingers below the edge of his cravat, the tickle of her nails on his skin sending chills down his spine and heat between his legs.

He ran his hands over her back and wrapped them around her waist, applying light pressure for a beat at its slimmest point. Her breath hitched when he sent his hands up along the swell of her breasts. When he dropped them to her backside, pulling her closer still, she gasped as the hardness in his pants pressed firmly into her belly. Cressida let her hands wander over his shoulders, down his arms, across his chest, exploring the muscled plains of his body, leaving a trail of fire as she went.

Lucius relinquished her mouth, dropping slow, purposeful kisses along her jaw, and pausing to flick and nip at her earlobe with his tongue before working his way down. When he moaned her name into the hollow of her neck, and she responded with a quiet, throaty 'yes' followed by another, he thought he might burst.

'Cressida.' He was panting as he pulled his mouth from her silky flesh. He studied the erratic rise and fall of her chest, her swollen lips, her clouded stare. Her hands remained on his chest, her fingers flexing and pressing against his waistcoat, while his rested at her waist.

'Cressida, I—' When her eyes met his, they were intent, searching, as if she was willing him to finish his thought. He swallowed. 'I—' The sound of Alexander's voice calling out from around the corner of the house fractured the alchemy of the moment.

They split apart, and Lucius was forced to return Cressida to the house where her aunt was waiting, but those precious minutes remained at the forefront of his mind. When he opened the book of poetry he'd purchased for her as a wedding gift, with the intention of writing a little something on the title page, it was that memory of her—pressing her body into his, running her tongue along his lips, looking at him with desire and anticipation and something more profound still—playing over and over again in the space behind his eyes which helped him find the words he couldn't that day in the garden.

To my wife on our wedding day—may we one day
find ourselves somewhere between these lines.

With love,
Lucius

21

*O*n Tuesday of the following week, the sun rose as it was wont to do and as it had for an endless number of days prior to this one. A maid entered to push open the heavy brocade curtains as she had every morning since Cressida arrived at Blackbird Hall. Cressida rubbed the sleep from her eyes and watched a rogue feather from the blanket she was burrowed under as it floated before her, descending from some unknown place.

She was not, as usual, thinking on how comfortable the bed was, how fine or inclement the weather beyond the long windows, or if she preferred coffee or tea that morning. Today, every thought was for her wedding, happening in—here she consulted the clock on the little table near the bed—four-and-a-quarter hours.

She had seen her intended several times since he kissed her the week before. Cressida, as she had often done since, reached up to touch her lips, as if doing so could recreate the sensation of his mouth on hers. It couldn't, of course, but thinking of him, how hard his body felt under her hands, how her nipples hardened when his hands cupped her breasts, how his lips on hers swept away reason and sense and left only a stir of something needy and vital in her belly.

Cressida wanted more of him, all of him.

She wanted to consume him as he did her, a feeling that both terrified and exhilarated her. Maybe most of all, she desperately wanted to know what it was he had been going to say before his brother interrupted. But with the wedding so near, whenever he came to call she was always surrounded— by sisters, by seamstresses, by people who seemed determined to prevent her and her bridegroom from sneaking a moment alone.

Instead, she had to settle for being the object of his intense gaze—the kind that raised the hair on her arms and sent shivers down her neck and back—and accept that his lips on the back of her hand when he departed was better than being without the feeling of his lips on her at all.

There had been no opportunity for a private exchange, for them to discuss what happened in the garden or to repeat the experience. Cressida pushed a cool hand to her cheek and used the other to throw off the bedclothes.

She had in recent days begun to understand herself, but she struggled still to reconcile the man who spoke to her with a callousness he seemed to save for moments when he wanted to be especially cutting with the man who very much seemed amenable to having her for a wife. A knock on the door interrupted her meditations and heralded the arrival of her aunt, who entered in front of a maid carrying a tray with coffee and biscuits.

'You aren't the first bride to wake up on her wedding day

without an appetite,' Aunt Delia said, seeing the frown on Cressida's face, 'but you'd be well-advised to have at least a nibble and some coffee.' She poured a cup of coffee for her niece and, after handing it over, reached for a small parcel on the tray. 'This came for you, delivered only ten minutes ago by a footman in familiar livery. Whatever it is can be of no concern to me. I'll leave you to open your intended's gift in private and have water sent up for a bath.'

When the door had clicked closed behind her aunt, Cressida picked up the package, turning it over in her hands before plucking at the green string wrapped around it. The brown paper fell away, revealing a book of poetry bound in beautiful soft brown leather, its title embossed in gold. She ran a reverent hand over the cover. As she opened it, her eyes caught immediately on the bold, defined penmanship of her almost-husband. Cressida had never seen his handwriting and was at first too absorbed in studying how the words looked to comprehend their meaning.

She read his note for a second time. It was only a salutation followed by one sentence—but the handful of words filled her lungs with air, her heart with hope, and her eyes with tears. She blinked them back as she flipped from page to page, reading one poem after the next. She consumed each more greedily than the last and stopped only when the tub had been filled.

His inscription was all she could think about when she entered the church—that, and the small feeling of possibility that had blossomed within her that morning. Something had shifted between them—she knew it must have for him to look at her as he did, kiss her as he did, for him to have written words turned towards a future full of promise.

Lord Windmere stood tall and proud at the altar, as dashing as ever in his grey superfine coat, and a waistcoat the colour of the pale pink blossoms on the Tamarisk trees of his estate that matched her dress.

He greeted her with a whispered compliment that she accepted with a shy smile. The ceremony was long, but Cressida was so occupied with the closeness of the man next to her, the changing of her situation, the impending realities of being a wife, that she heard not a word and lifted her brows in surprise when Mr Harland called for the ring. Despite the many uncertainties of the life she would now live, she felt no sadness and no regret when she signed *Ambrose* for the final time in the church register.

Her new husband assisted her into his curricle, and on the short ride to Blackbird Hall for the wedding breakfast, she wondered if he'd kiss her again, both wanting him to and being nervous he would. When he turned off onto an overgrown cart track and hid them out of sight, she knew that he would. Lord Windmere turned to her once the horses had come to a stop.

'Wife.' The word came out with reverence and a touch of disbelief.

Cressida met his eyes, trying to determine if what she saw in them was a reflection of what must be in her own. 'Husband.' Her voice was husky and hushed, the word foreign-feeling as it came out of her mouth.

He kept the reins in one hand and used the other to cup her cheek. The pad of his thumb trailed over her lips and then parted them. 'Wife.' There was nothing but desire in the word this time.

The irregular beat of her heart, the impossibility of drawing in a full breath, the knowledge that in another moment his lips would meet hers, prevented her from replying, and so she waited for one, two, three long seconds before he closed the distance between them.

His mouth was warm, and his kiss was light, teasing almost. With tentative, uncertain movements, she put her hands first on his chest and then snaked them around his back under his coat. Even with layers of fabric between them, she could feel the muscles in his back flexing under her gloved hands. He nipped at her bottom lip and used his tongue to request deeper access. Cressida had spent a sennight aching for this moment and matched his movements. When her own tongue flicked his upper lip, he moaned into her mouth. The sound, the vibration of his pleasure, rippled through her.

He broke the kiss, much to her dismay, and rested his forehead upon hers, his breath coming in short puffs that warmed her skin.

'We should continue on.'

She nodded against him.

When he pulled away from her, he did so with one last lingering look at her lips. With a flick of his wrists, they were moving once again.

There would be plenty of time after the wedding breakfast, Cressida told herself, to ask him what had changed and how and why and when—to figure out her own answers to those same questions. She wouldn't spoil this bright, clear day, which felt more like a wedding day between two people in love than two people who had never imagined themselves leg-shackled, much less to each other, with conversation sure to draw on unwanted and unwelcome memories.

Instead, she savoured the brush of his fingertips at the

small of her back when he was near, flushed the times she sought him out only to find his eyes focused on her from across the crowded room, and let herself bask in the knowledge that even though every neighbour in a five-mile radius was in attendance, his thoughts, his touch, his attention, were all hers.

22

*L*ucius came over to his wife's side as she spoke with one of the many guests at their decadent wedding breakfast. One look from the bridegroom and the other party retreated, leaving the newly married couple alone for a blessed few moments.

'Every eye in the room must be following us,' she ventured as he led her to the dessert table.

'Were you expecting something different?'

'Yes. No. I don't know.'

'You must acquit them of poor manners. I, too, find it impossible to take my eyes off you. You look otherworldly, Cressida.'

She peered up at him, her gaze dropping from his eyes to his lips, and he flexed the hand at his side. There was a moment not so long ago he'd asked her if she wished to be released from their engagement. In the seconds before she'd answered, his breath held and he acknowledged how wilfully blind he had been. If Lucius was feeling particularly honest with himself, he might go so far as to admit he'd been lost from the moment he saw her. His new wife, however, was a more complicated puzzle he could not figure out.

It crossed his mind once, in the middle of the night several days ago, that perhaps she'd sheathed her sword and accepted his attentions out of gratitude for him not calling off their engagement in light of her revelation. The idea disgusted him, and he wished to set it aside but couldn't just yet.

Today, when he'd pulled off the road on the way to Blackbird Hall, he'd done so with the intention of apologising for his past behaviour and asking how she wished to move forward in their marriage; he had laid himself bare in the book of poetry he'd sent to her that morning. Then he'd looked at her, her green eyes glowing in the white light of morning, and all he could think about was how his wife was the most beautiful creature in the world and how badly he needed to taste her. His mind was wandering the same road as they stood there together in front of cakes and tarts and pies of every sort.

'Lord Windmere, Lady Windmere.' Two of Miss Harland's brothers came forward to offer their congratulations, the elder exaggerating the 'Lady' part with a cheeky smile. As they slipped into comfortable conversation with Cressida, Lucius moved once more about the room and took up a post near his brother.

'It's unlikely you're fooling anyone, but you certainly cannot fool me, brother,' Alexander said, clapping Lucius on the back.

'Of what do you speak?'

'Luci, you may confess to me, if no one else, your feelings for your wife.'

Lucius thought of the words he'd written to her, how easily they'd come out, how truthful they were, how keen he was to protect their sentiment. 'I feel no more for my wife than is proper.'

'I believe that is a common symptom of a new love.'

Lucius didn't need to look towards his younger brother to know Alexander was smiling as he spoke.

'You need not say anything, Luci. No doubt you wish to protest, but then I'd be forced to call out your lie, so we might as well spare ourselves the scene. Ah, if you'll excuse me, a more pleasant companion has crossed my line of sight.' Alexander took himself off to engage the eldest Miss Ambrose.

Lucius watched him go. It wasn't long before his eyes found his bride once more. He took a deep breath, gathered his resolve, and took a step in her direction.

'My lord.'

A grating voice brought him to a stop, and he looked down to his right to see Mrs Davies.

'I offer my congratulations and those of Lady Lisle, who is back in London, as you know.'

He made no reply, agitated that his silence did nothing to stem the stream of words from her mouth.

'I see how taken you are with your bride. It's ever so charming when a husband is truly besotted with his wife. Of course, some credit must be given to the new Lady Windmere. She certainly has a way with Heaston men.'

Lucius felt like a fish in a pond. He could see the bait. He knew what would happen if he took it. 'You forget I'm an Anselme, ma'am.'

Mrs Davies tittered, a forced, practised sound. 'Ah.' She cut the air in front of her with her hand. 'Semantics. How a chit with no dowry and no connections could catch first the heir and then the marquess himself, well, I don't know if I ought to offer best wishes or ask for how-to suggestions for my own nieces.' She sniggered again.

'One catches disease, not husbands.' His face was impassive, his voice emotionless, concealing a mind that was whirling, trying to remember any mention of Cressida and James Heaston in the same sentence. As a man who could not enter a London drawing room without causing a wave of whispers and whose name appeared with considerable regularity in the newspapers, Lucius tended to let gossip wash over him without giving it the slightest attention. There was a memory niggling the back of his mind, though, and he wished the dammed woman would take herself away so he could think without her irksome voice thrumming in his ears.

'Oh, there's no need to be put out. It was darling, really, young love. She would always catch him up for a chat when she saw him in the village or let him escort her home. Of course, he had no choice but to break her heart. His mama would never have countenanced such a match. No offence intended, my lord. But I daresay none of that matters now that you two have each other. Oh, if you'll excuse me, I see Mrs Wicken.'

Lucius stood in her wake, completely still, jaw clenching and unclenching, hands clasped behind his back. Mrs Davies was a cat, and he dismissed her words outright. But as he watched his wife in conversation with her eldest sister, their heads bent together, the memory that had been on the fringes of his mind clarified. In the conversation he'd overhead the day he met Cressida she'd said she never wanted to see another Heaston; she'd called the family odious. She'd spoken with the same kind of rancour he'd heard in Lady Colchester's voice when he'd told her it was over between them.

'A turn in the garden?' he asked her, interrupting her discussion and taking hold of her elbow.

By the time they were alone outside, he could feel the blood throbbing in his veins. He was angry, irrationally so. He was agitated less by her withholding the information from him—after all, he would never enumerate his past relationships for her—than by the fact that she had given her heart to someone else before him, and to a scoundrel like the previous heir, no less, who, his lordship imagined, had done nothing to earn her regard.

He, meanwhile, had spent months in her company, nearly six weeks engaged, and had been married for several hours without yet knowing if she viewed him with any emotion warmer than indebtedness. He had revealed himself to her, and she had said nothing, made no acknowledgment of the book or what was written within, even now as he led them deeper into the garden. The greenery around him began to spin as an awful thought settled upon him. Perhaps she saw him simply as the closest thing she'd ever have to her first love.

'Was your measured dislike, your hesitation in marrying me, because you'd rather I was Viscount Torring?' he asked in a hard voice.

Cressida stumbled. 'I beg your pardon?'

'It was a clear enough question. He was your first love, was he not?'

Her eyes went wide, and a little storm brewed within them. Her mouth opened, but she made no response.

'All your fussing and fighting, all your talk about being forced into a marriage you don't want—it's not marriage you don't want, it's marriage to me, to a man who isn't your precious Viscount Torring.' His arm pulled as she attempted to wrench herself away from him, but he clasped her tighter to his side. 'No, you will not make a scene, and if you choose to do so, you will not care much for the consequences.'

Her cheeks and eyes were both bright with anger and hurt, his frenzied ire causing him to mistake the latter for embarrassment at being caught out.

'What is it you expect me to say, when you seem to have worked it all out yourself?'

'That's all the reply with which I'm to be gratified?'

'You've gratified yourself with false claims and have left no room for the truth in your one-sided dialogue.'

'I suppose if you wanted any part in this dialogue you would have been honest with me from the start.'

'Says the man who caused this whole situation with a lie.' She ripped her hand from where it was pinned to his side and spun to face him.

Even as he felt something inside himself tearing, he couldn't take his eyes off her. 'And what favours did you bestow upon him, ma'am? Were you as pliable under his caresses as you were mine?'

Cressida reached out to strike him, but he caught her wrist in a ruthless grasp.

'When I think of what a future with you must entail, I'm filled with equal parts shame for my own behaviour and revulsion at calling such a belligerent, cruel man husband.' She raised her chin as she spoke, and the words came out on a growl. 'You are the most disgusting, disagreeable creature I've ever had the misfortune to meet and undoubtedly will secure yourself as the greatest mistake of my life.'

'You've come to that conclusion several hours too late, madam.' He said so not with fury or resentment, but with the chilling indifference of one who has ceased to care.

She staggered a moment, as if struck, and her eyes, when they found his once more, were cloudy, like a lake after a storm.

'This was a mistake.' Her words were hushed and spoken neither to herself nor him. It didn't matter.

'Indeed. The mistake, as it always has been, remains mine.'

They returned to the house together at his insistence but remained only long enough to take their leave. At Tamarix, he ordered a tray to his room for dinner, ignored the sounds of his wife in the room adjoining his, and, before the sun crested the top of Dryce Hill the following morning, was on the road to London.

23

*C*ressida was miserable.

She'd spent half her night listening to the sounds of her new husband doing who knew what in his room, half the night with her head buried in her pillow keening until her throat was raw and ragged, and the entirety of the night regretting every decision she'd made that had brought her to where she was in that moment.

She struggled to grasp what had passed between them and failed to find a logical path that led from Lord Windmere kissing her, calling her beautiful, looking at her as if everything he longed for could be found in her eyes, to hurling hateful words at her. She couldn't understand how he'd ever thought her in love with someone else, much less with *that* man. She couldn't understand why, even if it had been true, it made him so angry. By the time she finally fell asleep, she felt as if she'd walked on stage in the middle of the third act of a play but hadn't seen the first two.

When she woke, there was one blessed minute where she forgot everything that had happened the previous day. Then she opened her eyes. The wall directly across from her was decorated with French-style panels of cream and gold that surrounded a fireplace so big she could nearly stand in it. The windows on the wall to the left were obscured by pale pink brocade tapestries that stretched at least twenty feet to pool on the floor.

She lay there, listening, hearing nothing except silence on the other side of the door that led to her husband's room. She knew he often rode out early and was grateful to have some little time to herself before facing him. With resignation, she pulled the bell, and when her maid Mary entered, she took a deep breath, and with a determination she didn't quite feel, asked the maid to bring a tray with coffee and whether she could provide the whereabouts of his lordship.

'I'm sure I'll come to know his habits soon enough, but I'd be quite indebted to you for a little guidance this morning.' Cressida added a smile that didn't reach her eyes. It was unusual, even she knew, for a bride and her groom to be apart the morning after their wedding, but Mary had made a favourable impression on Cressida when she met the maid the day she and Aunt Delia came for dinner. If this young woman was going to be her lady's maid, Cressida hoped they could forge a more personal connection, the kind that would allow her to ask questions to which she should already know the answer.

Mary's eyes dropped to the floor, her hands worrying each other.

'Mary?'

The maid looked up and her expression—one of alarm mingled with pity—made Cressida's heart plummet from her chest to her stomach.

'My lady,' Mary began with a quiver in her voice. The

address caught Cressida by surprise—she was now a lady, a *marchioness.*

'His lordship left for London early this morning, just after sunup.'

Cressida worked to keep her countenance and her reply even as she tamped down the dread rising within her. 'When is he expected back?'

Mary blinked rapidly and opened and closed her mouth several times before articulating a response. 'I'm sorry, my lady, he left no word of his return.'

The poor girl looked as if she was fighting to keep her lips from trembling. A maid shedding tears on Cressida's behalf was such an absurd thought, she had to swallow the uncomfortable giggle bubbling up within her. Her amusement was quickly replaced by anger, disappointment, an ache that overcame her whole body.

'I see. Thank you, Mary. Have the tray sent up, and I'll ring for you when I'm done.'

Even on her worst days at Red Fern Grange, Cressida was not the kind of young lady to upset herself, as far as that was possible, and so after breakfast, she took herself outside, resolved to think upon anything other than her husband abandoning her.

Her new brother, Mr Anselme, had left for Branford directly from the wedding breakfast. Her new aunt, who had removed to the dower house some days before the wedding, had taken her leave of them yesterday, although she would depart that morning, and no one would call on a new bride for some days. In short, there was nothing for Cressida to do but keep herself company and keep her mind off her situation. The first was easily done, the latter impossible.

She set off down a path at the southeastern corner of the

house. It skirted the manicured gardens and fountain just off the long wall of French doors and took her into a grove of cedar trees, their high green canopies dappling the light falling down around her. A twist or a turn would offer her a glimpse of the lake in the distance. With a sigh, she dropped to a little bench and pressed her palms into the cold stone on either side of her. She inhaled a deep, slow breath, her nose filling with the warm, slightly spicy fragrance of the trees, the taste of their woodiness on her tongue.

With her eyes closed, her head turned up to the sky, one lone tear snaked down her cheek. That was all she would allow herself. She swiped at it and blinked her eyes open, focusing on the wide trunks of the trees. She envied their purpose, their repose, their ignorance. She remained in that attitude, still and silent and solemn, until the sound of a throat clearing somewhere behind her intruded.

Lord Windmere's aunt was standing a short distance away. 'I beg pardon for the intrusion.'

'Not at all, ma'am,' Cressida said, patting her cheeks and eyes before rising and smoothing her skirts.

'You ought to call me Aunt Bea. Make room.' She waggled her walking stick in Cressida's direction and came nearer, the stick leaving little imprints in the dirt path.

Cressida resumed her seat but said nothing, could think of nothing to say which would not somehow betray her situation, her emotions.

'I had not thought to see you this morning.'

'No.' The one word came out quietly. To have said it any louder would be to give away the tremor in her voice.

'I was on my way to the main house to leave a letter for you before I depart.' Aunt Bea said as she pulled the letter from a pocket in her dress.

'You need not leave so soon. His lordship, I'm sure, has already said as much.'

Aunt Bea seemed to consider her next words. 'Young couples need their space. Even a dower house may feel too close before long.'

'Space doesn't seem to be an issue.' Again there was a long pause, and Cressida began to sense the woman next to her already knew his lordship was away from home. 'He left. This morning.'

A noncommittal murmur came from beside her.

'He *left*.' Cressida repeated it, but this time her voice splintered like bark tearing from a tree. Her chest compressed, and she turned her head away, embarrassed by her want of composure. A hand, its fingers heavy with rings, came to rest on her shoulder, and together the pair sat like that until Cressida excused herself, fleeing to the relative safety of her rooms.

But her thoughts could rest on nothing—they jumped from the moment she met Lord Windmere to the moment he kissed her, from the time he patted her back as she coughed, as if it were the most natural gesture in the world, to the time he burst into her father's study. Always, her mind came back to their argument, to the words he said before he left: the mistake was his.

Her emotions fluctuated in the same tumultuous manner: from anger to embarrassment, gratitude to despair, and somewhere deeper still, a feeling she'd only just begun to discover within herself. In this spiritless state, she passed her first several days at Tamarix Hall, and would have been content to waste away slowly in her room had she not been interrupted on the third day of her self-imposed confinement by a stern-faced Aunt Bea.

'I thought you were for Mr Anselme's?'

Aunt Bea cast her a keen once-over, taking in the dark circles under Cressida's eyes, her pallor. 'And allow you to waste away up here and give your husband cause to take me to task? Which, when he eventually returns, he surely would do.'

Cressida felt a protest on her lips but remained silent.

'If there isn't already talk in the village, there will be soon enough. It may be impossible to quash, but we can temper it.' Aunt Bea came further into the room and seated herself in one of the velvet chairs near the fireplace. 'We'll call on your aunt tomorrow, and Mrs Hobbs as well. You'll send word for your sisters to come and take tea and dinner here with us. We'll make it known you're ready for callers, and when they come, you'll say something about the many responsibilities of a marquess and your role in supporting him how best you can, which currently means overseeing his new estate.'

Cressida agreed, mostly thinking it the quickest way for her to be left alone once again, but Aunt Bea, in tones one might use with a naughty child, ordered her new niece downstairs for coffee, cards, and a walk in the garden if the clouds cleared—anything, the lady said, to return the bloom to Cressida's cheeks and prevent the servants from having more to gossip about.

24

*L*ucius pushed Helios hard on the road to London, hoping to outrun his guilt, his discomfiture, the pain that had seeped in and settled heavy in his heart before he could recognise the feeling.

All he'd wanted was for Cressida to deny the claims made by Mrs Davies—whether true or not. But she hadn't. She'd met his anger with her own, and as she issued one recrimination against him after another, she never spared a breath to disavow her feelings for another man. And what recriminations they'd been. She'd called him disgusting, cruel, a mistake. The memory of her resentful face caused the ember of outrage in him to flame once more. He was none of those things, but that she'd married a man of whom she thought so little could only reflect poorly on her own character.

His mind had not found pleasanter topics on which to dwell by the time he arrived at his home in Brook Street, but the season was well underway, and he had every intention of throwing himself into the amusements it offered for several weeks, before continuing on to visit another property that came with the title, one situated on the coast near Torquay.

When he called on Lord and Lady Dane the following morning, the muscle in his jaw was still pulsing. His two friends exchanged a concerned sidelong glance, and Lady Dane went so far as to ask if they'd have the pleasure of meeting his new wife. Lucius's curt one-word answer— 'No'—was enough to silence her on the subject, but he remained under careful observation by both occupants of the house.

In their company that evening, he found himself at a soirée hosted by the Seftons, and he had hardly entered before everyone in the room knew both that the former Mr Anselme was present *and* without his new lady wife. Mrs Reading, a widow in the middle of her thirties, who looked as fresh-faced as a girl in her first season, was the first to try her luck with London's favourite rake.

He had not seen her since before her husband's death a little more than a year ago, and he bowed over her hand when she joined the little group with which he stood.

'My lord, you and I have something in common,' she said, with a wide smile that showed a row of perfectly straight teeth.

'Don't keep me in suspense.'

'We both return to society a little altered: me as a widow, you a married man.'

He nodded once.

'Tell me, is your new wife a beauty? She must be.' As she spoke, she hooked her hand onto his arm and turned him a little away from the others.

Lucius's gaze lost focus for half a minute as he pictured Cressida's ethereal face turned up at him and imagined himself fifty miles away in a strawberry garden. 'She is. Very much so.'

'And yet,' replied she, peeping up at him through her long lashes, her big brown eyes full of studied innocence, 'you are here.'

'My presence in London suits the both of us quite well at present.'

She tipped her head towards him and said in a quiet, purring voice. 'Undoubtedly your presence in town must increase my own pleasure in being here.'

He felt the squeeze on his arm before she disengaged to greet some other friend. It was a calculated move, one meant to increase his interest. That lady kept her distance the rest of the evening, but he could feel her eyes on him. When once he glanced her way, she bestowed upon him a small, guileless smile at odds with the gown she wore, cut low enough to advertise her best assets.

As it happened, Lucius crossed paths with Mrs Reading several more times in that same week. Once when he walked home from his solicitor's office, once in the park, where she was squired around by some young buck, and once at a private ball, where she mentioned a painting in a salon at the end of the hall she thought he might like to see.

'I'm afraid I've no interest in art this evening.'

One arched eyebrow jumped a very little, but she merely inclined her head and moved away.

'Redheads never were your type.'

A hard little smile played on Lucius's lips as he looked over to see Lady Colchester at his side, her raven hair shimmering in the candlelight, her hazel eyes alive with interest and desire.

'I hope you've no comb hidden in your skirts.'

'Would you like to check for yourself?' she said, with a

delicate laugh. 'Dear me. Old habits and all that. How good it is to see you again, my lord.'

'Is it? I hadn't thought you'd feel so.'

'Come,' she drew the word out, 'there could never be hard feelings between us, and now that you've returned...' She let the insinuation hang in the air between them for several seconds. 'Oh, there's Prudence Calloway. You'll excuse me, but think on what I said.' She bid him goodbye as she walked away.

He did think on what she said, for most of the night. Lady Colchester had been a spirited and adventurous lover, but he did not feel that pull to her that he once did. She was still lovely as ever, though, and his own wife had already cast him off. In fact, she already assumed he'd take a mistress and seemed unlikely to care one way or another what he was doing. The thought was meant to bolster him, but it only brought on a melancholy that persisted until he fell asleep.

On Wednesday, he saw Lady Colchester at Almack's. He refrained from dancing entirely but went so far as to let her make use of his arm to escort her to the refreshment table.

As his party was donning their coats and waiting for the carriage, a set of long, slender fingers, those of an exceptional pianoforte player, closed around his wrist, followed by a hissed 'Lucius.'

'Yes, Almeria?'

'What is it you think you're doing?'

'Returning home for better drink than can be found here. After you, my dear.' He left her no space to reply, although it was not as if the conversation she wished to have could be held in the entryway to Almack's in any case.

If he thought that had put paid to it, he was mistaken. On Thursday, well before the appropriate hour for morning calls,

Lady Dane swept into his house, telling the butler, the footman, and anyone else standing in the hallway that his lordship had exactly a quarter of an hour to present himself in his own drawing room or she would see herself upstairs.

The servants at Lord Windmere's London residence were too familiar with Lady Dane, who often acted as lady of the house in absence of any other, to be surprised by the command. The footman took himself up the stairs without waiting for confirmation from the butler.

'To what do I owe the pleasure?' Lucius asked, closing the door of the drawing room behind him exactly thirteen minutes after Almeria's arrival.

'This visit will be anything but pleasurable for you, Luci. You've been married little more than a fortnight—and Lady Colchester? Bloody hell, Lucius.'

He fought a small smile. Lady Dane was a paragon of propriety, except she'd developed a fondness for swearing early on, thanks to a pack of elder brothers. She only ever did so in private, but it was one of the things her husband liked best about her.

'My wife prefers my absence at present.'

She pinned him with an unrelenting stare. 'What did you do to her?'

'You take her side? You don't even know her.'

'No, not at all, but I know you. I have done more than half my life. I know what you've been through. I know what it cost you. I know what you think you want and what you really want. I know you've two paths before you, and you may even now have already chosen wrong. I know you deserve happiness. I know your marriage deserves a chance. And I know your wife deserves better than being made the fool.'

'Even if I was not extended the same courtesy?'

Almeria gave a sad little shake of her head. 'You've never been an eye-for-an-eye kind of gentleman, Luci. You wouldn't be you if you were.' The two of them had remained standing, one too tense to sit and the other too worried. Her tone changed when she spoke next. 'Lady Lisle has had much to say on the subject.'

'She has much to say on everything. She's gifted in such a way as that.'

'She wouldn't and couldn't—'

Lucius's handsome features hardened. 'If you intend to use the rest of that sentence to rebuke me, you may as well swallow it.'

'If you behaved like you had even a single care for your new wife—'

'You've never been presumptuous. I recommend you not start now, Almeria.'

'Cut it, Luci. It's not presumption, it's observation.' Her voice never rose, never quivered with emotion, but he sensed the anger underscoring each word.

'Almeria—' All the irritation faded from his body when he saw real concern on his dear friend's face.

She shook her head. 'No. Let us say no more on it for today. I cannot bear us to part with any remnant of rancour, and I'm wanted at a charity meeting.' To make her point, she crossed from her position at the far end of the room, squeezed both of his hands, kissed his cheek, and saw herself out without another word.

When she had gone, he called for his carriage and went directly to Curzon Street. The look on Lady Lisle's face when he was announced was one of surprise, as he had not waited for the butler to return but rather followed in his wake.

'Fortuitous I find you alone and at your leisure, ma'am.

Fashionable ladies always seem to have new gowns to order, new friends to visit.'

'Indeed,' she replied, eyeing him with equal parts hesitation and speculation. 'To what do I owe the pleasure?'

'It's come to my attention that you've quite strong opinions on my marriage. I thought I'd present myself to you, so you may share your thoughts directly with the party involved.'

She sniffed once. 'I've no more to say on the subject than anyone else.'

'You ought to have nothing to say at all.'

'I only discuss what I see, which, by the by, is just what I told your wife would happen were she foolish enough to wed you. Your behaviour, Lord Windmere, is not exceptional by any means, although your return to Lady C's side could not go unnoticed.'

The only outward sign that her words affected him in the least was the one quick clench of his fist and the slight flare of his nostrils. 'It must be excruciating, madam, to address me by the title first meant for your husband and then your son. Worse still must be living with the knowledge that a young lady from the country, with no fortune, no connections, now bears the title you undoubtedly coveted even before you married Lord Lisle.'

He stepped further into the room, noting that when he did so her shoulders went stiff. 'How is it, pray tell, to imagine her giving directions for dinner, visiting tenants who were never as glad to see you, redecorating the rooms you yourself may have had if fate had not intervened? How does it feel, knowing everything you wanted, everything you thought you would have, is now hers?'

Lady Lisle's cheeks reddened with fury, and her jaw moved as though she was grounding down rocks between her teeth.

'Whatever you feel for her is nothing compared to what you'll feel towards me if you continue to discuss my marriage and besmirch my wife.'

'Is that so? And what will you do, my lord? You cannot fleece me of my fortune at the card table, you cannot send the runners after me for the crime of *besmirching* your wife, you cannot meet me at dawn.'

Lucius could tell the woman was beginning to feel revived, as ladies like her often did in the face of what they considered an empty threat. It was just as he intended. 'Quite right, ma'am. I can do none of those things. I am, in fact, very limited in how I may act. But you've forgotten, perhaps, that while I've ascended to a marquisate, I retain roots in trade, and they run deep.' There was an almost undetectable narrowing of her eyes. 'With very little effort on my part, I can prevent you from purchasing your favourite silks, muslins, lace, ribbons, boots. I can prevent you from getting new stone for your floors, rugs for your drawing rooms, tables, chairs, drapes, mirrors, clocks, tea, jewels, bone china—in short, anything and everything. If you keep your tongue in your mouth, perhaps I'll let you have Cheapside.'

'You couldn't.'

'I can, and I will.' He had no more to say on the subject, and so bade Lady Lisle good day, ignoring the outraged blustering behind him as he let himself out of her drawing room.

TWO WEEKS LATER, he numbered one of a large party at Vauxhall Gardens. And when his party joined with Lady Colchester's, he allowed himself, when everyone was sufficiently distracted, to be led along one of the dark pathways on the edge of the gardens.

When both park-goers and the accompanying noise faded to a hush, she brought him to a stop in a dark, far-off row of trees, and reached her face up to his, wrapping her hands around his neck. 'How I've wanted you,' she whispered into the dark as she pulled his mouth to hers.

Lucius ran his hands over the bodice of her dress, eliciting a moan, but when she reached for the fall of his pants, as she'd done many times before, he jumped back, putting an arm's length between them.

Lady Colchester's eyes were curious, her pink lips parted, her chest heaving. He shook his head, as if trying to block out his wife's face, which appeared whenever he closed his eyes. He stepped forward and Lady Colchester pressed herself fully against him. He cupped her backside through layers of silk, pulling her up against the hardness constrained by his breeches. She reached down between them, taking what she could of him into her hand and rubbing him through the fine fabric.

'No.' Lucius wasn't sure if he was saying that to her, himself, the voices in his head or all three as he thrust her away from him.

'When did you become coy, my lord? It's a new game I quite like.' She advanced towards him once more and he stepped around her.

'You mistake me, ma'am.'

'There is no mistaking what you want,' Lady Colchester replied, her eyes dipping below his waist.

'What I want isn't here.'

Her amorous gaze faltered a little then, but she reached a hand up to trail across the rise of her breasts. 'Come now,

Lucius. Haven't I always been able to give you what you want?'

He stiffened at her familiar use of his name. Whatever disgust his wife felt for him was nothing compared to what he currently felt for himself. He did not recognise the man who stood in the garden, the one he'd become on his wedding day: petty, jealous, callous.

He took another step away from her. 'Good evening, Lady Colchester.'

'Lucius!' she cried out, her hand reaching for him.

'Lord Windmere, ma'am,' was all the reply he gave as he retreated.

He left London the following morning after penning two letters. One to his steward in Torquay delaying his arrival indefinitely, and one to Almeria that contained just two words: *Thank you.*

Not for a single moment, from the time Lucius arrived in London to the time he left, had he considered the possibility that any report of his behaviour would reach his wife.

25

*C*ressida woke up, took breakfast in her room, read a book in the conservatory, called on tenants in the company of Aunt Bea, visited Blackbird Hall, walked to Dryce Hill with her sisters and Sophia, and went to the Smiths' twice weekly to keep up with the children's arithmetic lessons—in short, she spent her days not totally unlike those before her wedding, except in this new chapter of her life, she was aware of a nagging unhappiness.

She maintained her composure when around her sisters so as to give them no cause for worry. How easily the lie slipped out when she told them her husband had urgent business that recalled him to town so soon. But when she was alone, tucked into her own little corner of the world, Cressida would torture herself by reading and rereading poems from the book he gave her, imagining what it would be like if he was there, whispering the words in her ear, his breath hot on her neck, his teeth nipping at her earlobe. It always ended the same—with her pushing the heels of her palms to her eyes and holding in every sob and wail and whimper.

In the weeks since her husband had left, she'd had ample time to consider their last exchange, ample time to regret the role she'd played and how easily she'd allowed anger to overcome her. She could have told him the truth; undoubtedly she should have. Had not her sister advised her to do so some time ago? It had been within her power to relieve him of whatever misapprehension or misunderstanding was at the root of his struggle, and she had chosen not to. Did not that make her the cruel one?

He'd not sent one letter. He'd not forgiven her, but she was ready to ask for his forgiveness and to extend her own should he wish it.

Cressida could hardly attend to Mrs Peregrine or to Miss Fox before her and made up her mind that when the last of her callers had gone, she would write to her husband and request his presence at Tamarix. She had hurled whatever biting thing she could at him, but in her heart, she knew him to be thoughtful, fair, and considerate. Just as she knew herself to have been unjust and unkind from the moment they met.

Her dislike of his relations and her own experience with them had formed the basis of her opinion of him, and she'd actively worked to remain entrenched in her position even as evidence proved him an attentive estate owner and pleasant neighbour. When she considered that a man with his looks, wealth, and position had veritably thrown himself away on a country nobody to save her reputation, her selfishness, her conceit, took the wind from her lungs. If he was not willing to extend the forgiveness she sought, she had no one to blame but herself.

First she must write to him. He would come—she knew in her bones he would—whatever he thought of her. And although she didn't know what would happen after, nothing could happen until they were together once more.

With that settled, she tried to refocus on the conversation at hand. Mrs Peregrine was across from her in the green drawing room, chattering on about a new novel, *Sense and Sensibility*, which Cressida had yet to read.

'Mrs Davies,' Yates announced, drawing the attention of the two ladies already present.

'How charming you look, my dear. The title certainly suits you.'

'Thank you, ma'am. Won't you be seated?' Cressida replied, in as bland a tone as she could manage. Sitting for callers, particularly those who came only for the spectacle of seeing Miss Cressida Ambrose in the role of lady of the manor, was one of her least favourite things about her marriage so far.

'The title will have to be some consolation, I suppose,' Mrs Davies said, taking the chair near Mrs Peregrine, 'when his lordship is running wild in London.'

Cressida saw the aghast look on Mrs Peregrine's face— whether from the information or the blatant rudeness, she couldn't be sure, but she refused to mirror it. 'You seem to have more insight into Lord Windmere's doing than myself, ma'am, but naturally my husband's letters would omit any intimations of his running wild.' Another lie that rolled off her tongue with startling ease.

'Perhaps "wild" is too strong a word. He's only doing what so many other men do. Although most wait until they've at least sired an heir.'

'Back in your box, Miss Sharp,' Mrs Peregrine interjected with no little antipathy, but it was too late. Cressida was silent as she willed the red stains on her cheeks to fade away with all her might, knowing the effort was futile.

'Oh, please, Penelope,' Mrs Davies replied, as nonchalantly as one might when debating whether the day would be sunny or cloudy. 'No one expected a man of his reputation to do otherwise, least of all his wife, I'm sure. It's in all the papers, he and Lady Colchester, and no surprise there, either. Naturally I assumed our dear Lady Windmere must have known. Everyone else does.' She turned towards Cressida, and said with false care, 'It's no big thing, dear, but this is why you must expand your circle.'

'To include you?' snorted Mrs Peregrine.

Mrs Davies ignored her. 'You'll have eyes and ears everywhere, crucial to knowing the latest *on dits* and to avoid being taken unawares, as you were today.'

'A kindness, ma'am,' replied Cressida, with a frostiness befitting her new station as she rose, signalling an abrupt end to the unwelcome visit.

Mrs Peregrine gave her a quick squeeze of the hand and left with Mrs Davies, but Cressida remained standing, unsure what to do with herself and paralysed by the torrent of emotions coursing through her body. She was mortified, devastated, jealous. Despite him telling her he would do as much, she felt betrayed, even though she had no right to be. He had been clear from the beginning who he was.

She wanted to hie off to London and confront him; she wanted to remain at Tamarix and upset his household in every possible way; she wanted to disappear and live a life other than her own. Instead, she stormed from one side of the room to the other. She stormed up the stairs to her chambers. And she tore to shreds sheets of blank paper just so something else might absorb the restless energy pulsing through her.

Cressida wasn't home to visitors the rest of the day and spent it instead being angry with Lord Windmere for forcing her into a fake engagement and a fake marriage, and with herself for tying herself forever to a man who thought only of himself when all she'd thought about since the day she met him was him.

She pulled the bell, and when Mary answered her summons, she asked if Lord Windmere was in the habit of reading the papers. The maid answered that the papers were delivered and laid out for him with his breakfast, but whether he read them or not she could not say for certain.

'And in his absence?'

'Mr Yates keeps a months' worth at a time, I believe.'

'Bring them to me.'

A look of apprehension pulled at Mary's features. 'Which ones, ma'am?'

'All of them. As many as are available.'

Mary did as she was bid and when she left once more, having deposited a stack of newspapers on the little table between the chairs near the fireplace, Cressida threw herself into scanning the society pages: *LW and MR seen at Sefton Soirée; LW and LC rekindling London's worst-kept secret; LW taken up by LC in Hyde Park; LW and LC disappear into the dark at Vauxhall.* Her heart clenched so hard she unconsciously brought a hand up to rub her chest before clawing at the pages in front of her, unaware she was sobbing as she ripped apart every mention of her husband with another woman.

'Cressida, are you—?' Aunt Bea came to an abrupt stop in the doorway. 'What's all this?'

Cressida turned, not bothering to wipe her eyes or offer an explanation but panting out the question at the forefront of her mind: 'Who's Lady Colchester? Her initials are on every stupid page with his. Who is she?' Her voice rose to a fever pitch, her limbs were shaking, her eyes burning. '*Who* is she?'

The older lady had by now noticed the shredded newspapers on the floor. She sucked in her lips and let enough time lapse to signal the internal debate she was waging with herself. After several excruciating minutes standing in silence, Aunt Bea finally said, 'Lady Colchester was his mistress before he came to Tamarix Hall.'

Cressida's legs buckled and she crumpled to the ground, head buried in her hands, body wracked with silent sobs, the kind that left no doubt in her mind or others about her true feelings for her husband.

'This will never do,' Aunt Bea said on a sigh.

Around her, Cressida heard the swish of skirts, the rustle of paper, Mary's worried voice when she came into the room, and Aunt Bea's reply.

'Stoke the fire, Mary. It's beneath your position, but you understand the necessity. Then toss this rubbish in. All of it. Then you'll need to pack a valise for her ladyship. The length of her trip remains undetermined, but you'll do your best. Oh, and discover Mrs Yates's whereabouts and send her to me immediately. Do that first.'

Cressida hardly noticed what was happening around her. She pulled herself from the floor long enough to crawl under her bedcovers, oblivious to the dismayed look on Aunt Bea's face, and was in the same position when Mary returned with the housekeeper.

'Mrs Yates, unless I'm much mistaken, we've an ally in you.'

The housekeeper's look flitted from the papers Mary was gathering to Cressida curled in her bed. 'That word brings war to mind, ma'am.'

'How sagacious you are. Can you be depended upon?'

'Of course!' exclaimed Mrs Yates, in the tones of someone who'd been greatly offended.

'I'm here to take my leave. Tomorrow morning, I depart before breakfast. Mary will bring Cressida her breakfast tray as usual—it's imperative she's seen after I leave—but then you and Mary here must contrive to sneak her out. I'll be waiting on the western road at the edge of the property just beyond the Temple of Diana. Cressida will leave a letter addressed to you to put you above suspicion. It's imperative, as I think you both have puzzled out, not to say a word about her whereabouts.'

Both women, sparing doleful looks for the lady of the house, swore their agreement and finessed the following day's plans.

26

*E*ach hour on the road from London to Tamarix that brought Lucius closer to the life he wanted to live also brought clarity on what he would do and say to prove himself worthy of the woman he'd married.

He couldn't recall a time in his life he'd felt so anxious, so uncertain. The very idea she might refuse to hear his apologies, that she might reject him out of hand, was as possible as it was terrifying.

By the time he turned through the north gates and down the tree-lined drive that ran in a long straight line from the road to the entrance of the manor, his relief at being home was entirely eclipsed by the unease thrumming through every vein, every muscle, every bone holding his body together.

Lucius handed Helios over to one of the grooms and strode up the two dozen steps of the entrance, his nerves increasing with each one. Yates greeted him as if his arrival was an expected event.

'Yates, where might I find my wife at this hour?' He

couldn't change, couldn't wash or refresh himself or do anything until he'd seen her.

The butler cleared his throat.

'Is there something amiss?'

'In a manner of speaking, my lord.'

Lucius resisted the urge to run an impatient hand over his face. 'Where is her ladyship?'

Yates replied in a bland voice. 'Her ladyship is unavailable.'

The words were measured, and for the first time, Lucius noticed a worried crease forming on Yates's stony countenance.

'We've got on quite well, you and I, but that will change unless you find the words to adequately answer my question.'

An audible swallow preceded the butler's reply. 'The thing is, sir, I cannot say where she is.'

'You cannot say?' Lucius took one menacing step closer. To his credit, Yates didn't recoil. 'What is it you aren't telling me?'

'No, my lord, I cannot say where she is. You have my apologies.'

'I've no interest in your apologies. What aren't you telling me? Where is Cressida?' Lucius's voice went from a whisper to a roar, fed by panic that came on like a summer squall. 'Lady Windmere has been away from home, my lord, for nearly a sennight. We were under the impression you must know, given the duration of her absence and the—the—nature of her departure.'

Lucius's blue-green eyes sharpened, and his words came out strained. 'A sennight?'

'Yes, my lord. I cannot say with any certainty, my lord, but I don't believe she remains in the county.'

'That girl has hardly been past the lookout, and you

without a clue or care to the whereabouts of your mistress? I consider myself a generous employer, Yates, but you are sorely trying me. What if she's been kidnapped or is injured and abed in some dingy inn?'

'To that end, you can rest easy, my lord. No one in the house saw her go, but she left a note on her mantelpiece for Mrs Yates.'

'Send Mrs Yates to me—and that note—straightaway.'

Lucius brushed past his butler and went straight for his study, without a care for the dust on his boots or his person.

He paced, running one hand and then the other through his thick hair, picking up the decanter and setting it down, vacillating between the desire to seek liquid comfort and knowing he needed to keep his head about him at least a little longer.

He picked up the small but heavy sculpture on the corner of the desk that had belonged to his grandfather. It was a snail with a silver-gilt shell; perched atop was a small rider, bow in one hand, reins in the other. It was an odd piece, but one Lucius loved. He ran his thumb along the shell. For a moment, the frenzy within him stilled.

Time stretched on as he waited for Mrs Yates, and a quick glance at the clock when she finally came bustling through the study door revealed it had hardly been ten minutes. He held his hand out in silence for the letter, which was dutifully placed in it without comment or question.

Mrs Yates,

You have my apologies for making off like a thief in the night with a bag full of silver. It's come to my attention that my presence is needed elsewhere, and I must depart with all expe-

diency, and, indeed, some secrecy (but not the silver). You
may assure his lordship, when or if he returns, that I am well.
You have my gratitude for all you do in the running of
Tamarix Hall.

Lady Windmere

'This is it?' he asked as he reread *when or if he returns*. His
stomach dropped. His wife thought so little of him that she
believed herself abandoned, forsaken, without a word from
him; with sickening swiftness, he realised that was exactly
what he had done. Remorse and self-loathing washed over
him like a wave threatening to pull him out to sea. He was a
coward—a coward who would be served his just deserts if his
wife never reappeared. 'Mrs Yates, you are a woman with ears
to the ground. You haven't heard a murmur about her whereabouts? Are you certain she's not simply residing at Blackbird
Hall?'

Mrs Yates pinched her lips in a compassionate frown. 'I
called at Blackbird Hall myself, my lord, after receiving that
letter in your hands. Mrs Wright assured me the young
mistress is well, but with her agreement, I put it out that she's
off visiting some of your family, being a new bride and all. It
would be an oddity for her to do so without her bridegroom,
but if the village folk don't take a pet with that detail, who am
I to point it out to 'em?'

'Have my horse brought round.'

Lucius waited for Mrs Yates to leave before letting the
curses free from his mouth. He had no one with whom to be
upset besides himself and felt, without qualification, that he
deserved every tormenting moment. When his horse was
saddled, he rode directly to see Cressida's aunt.

'Through here, my lord,' the butler at Blackbird Hall said, leading Lucius to the familiar sitting room. Cressida's aunt stood from her perch on the settee, her eldest niece next to her, and as he walked in, he could feel his presence in the room push out all the air.

'Lord Windmere. Welcome back. Would you care for tea?'

'Will the leaves reveal my wife's whereabouts?'

Astrid lowered her head to stare at her clasped hands. Mrs Wright, on the other hand, studied him as if deciding how much he was worthy of knowing.

'If Cressida didn't see fit to share her whereabouts with you, neither can I.'

'But you know where she is?'

There was a long pause.

'Yes.'

'Tell me.' The words shot out like a bullet from a gun. He added, with all the depth of emotion he felt, 'Please.'

Aunt Delia's expression softened; the marshal light in her eyes was replaced with something like condoling warmth. Still, however, she refused and retook her seat.

Lucius remained standing. 'Will you at least tell me if she's all right? She's well?' He wondered if Aunt Delia could hear the desperation in his voice.

'She's well, yes.'

'Where is she?'

'You can ask as many times as you'd like, but unless she advises me otherwise, my answer must remain the same.'

He dropped into a chair, rubbing both hands over his face and through his already mussed hair. 'Will you tell her I returned and that I hope she will come home as well?' His voice cracked with raw emotion.

'I will.' It wasn't Cressida's aunt, but her sister who spoke.

When he turned his head in her direction, he was treated to a small smile—not the pitying kind, but the kind that gave him the smallest amount of hope.

When he returned to Tamarix Hall, he went, for the first time, into his wife's rooms. Despite the time that had passed since she last occupied the space, her scent was everywhere. The soft notes of honey and lavender could almost fool him into thinking she had just swept through.

He ran a hand along her dressing table, noting that her brush was gone, although several pretty hair combs remained. He sat in a chair near the empty fireplace where he imagined she sat to read while her hair dried after a bath. He didn't even know what her hair looked like out of its pins, but imagined it long and thick, tumbling in soft curls around her slender shoulders.

His eyes landed on a slim book, the one he'd given her on their wedding day, resting on her bed as if cast off. It called to him, and he picked it up reverently, as if it might turn to dust in his hands. There were passages underlined, some even annotated, and he took a seat in the chair near the window to read through some of the poems.

Lucius returned to the first page at the front, saw his own words mocking him. Words he'd meant then and meant still. Words that reminded him what an unmitigated arse he'd been.

How long had it taken him to perceive his own feelings? And what had he expected of her? To know her own heart as quickly as he knew his own? He had been the object of her warm gaze, he had felt her moan against him, felt her tentative touch become certain. He had written his words, not with expectation, but because they were honest, and then he'd used her silence as an excuse to hurt her after she unknowingly and unwittingly hurt him.

He set the book down but found himself often returning to it in the days after his return. He had his own copy, but his copy didn't have her even lines, her hand on the pages throughout.

There, in his wife's room, Lucius finally began to understand his father, how helpless he must have felt watching his wife slowly fade away, and how hollow he must have felt once she was gone.

27

'Well, dear, what is it?'

Cressida turned her head up at the sound, but she missed what was said. Aunt Bea looked at her expectantly.

'Sorry. Did you say something?' She glanced back down at the letter in her hands. *Your husband is returned and desirous of seeing you.* 'He is once more at Tamarix.'

'I see.' A long stretch of silence followed. 'Would you like to go home?'

'Yes.' The word came out before Cressida had time to think. 'No. I don't know.' A part of her was desperate to return, to run into the house and throw herself into the arms that felt made to hold her. She wanted to run her fingers through his hair, which she now knew was soft as goose down, and along his stubborn jaw. She wanted him to entwine their fingers as he had that night in her aunt's library and to look at her as if he meant to eat her whole.

The sentence in her sister's letter, when she first read it, sent happiness coursing through her, until she remembered that he'd left the morning after the wedding and returned to his mistress, an unfortunate fact that broke her heart over and over again. It was possible, she had to admit to herself, that he may not wish to sweep her up into his arms. He could be wishing her home in order to announce his intention of living mostly in London, or his plan to send her away, or to demand the marriage be annulled. He could do a thousand things that would destroy her. Time and distance had tempered the most passionate feelings that had overwhelmed her, but she was not ready to return. She could not face him until she knew herself capable of weathering whatever might be the outcome of their meeting.

'When you decide, you tell me.'

Cressida nodded and allowed her mind to wander once more. Her week in the dower house at Branford had passed slowly. When they'd first rumbled down the drive, she couldn't help but to think of how he had described his long-time home. Charming was the perfect word for it. Despite its size, it had a cosy quality, thanks to the vines running up one half of its façade and the flowers blooming in every colour, visible from nearly every angle. She'd found herself wondering where his mother's strawberry field was, the thought sending a burst of pink to her cheeks.

Mr Anselme—Alexander as she now called him—had been surprised to see them both.

'Are you?' Aunt Bea had asked, and his grimace had said more than any other reply could. 'And I thought you were in the habit of reading the papers with your coffee in the morning. I'd not believed us a family of fools, but'—she let the word rest a moment—'naturally you know nothing.'

'Aunt.' There was a hint of reproof in the single syllable.

'Don't "Aunt" me. Your brother won't suffer more than is

good for him from this little trick. On the contrary, it will do him a great deal of good to think her lost. You men so often don't know what you want till you cannot have it.'

He'd turned to look at Cressida and addressed her directly. 'He is the best of brothers. I hope it's not too late for him to prove himself the best of husbands.'

Cressida did not feel so sure but kept that to herself. They'd seen little of Alexander in the days since; Cressida suspected he felt guilty keeping such a secret from his brother and could not fault him for that. The lack of his presence suited her quite well as she alternated between moments of nothingness and moments of deep sorrow and interminable longing. She read, she slept, she arranged flowers, she worked in the little herb garden, and she made contradictory wishes as she let one week fade into the next.

She had said nothing regarding her husband when she next wrote her sister, but half hoped and half feared a repeat of his sentiment when she broke the seal on Astrid's most recent letter, which she'd picked up from the salver on coming in from the garden, a basket of tulips hanging from her arm.

'No. Oh no, no. No.' Cressida chanted the word as she dropped the basket to the ground and ran through the hall, peering into two parlours before she found Aunt Bea in the bright morning room at the back of the house. 'We must go at once—please. It's Cora. She's been a little sick since she got caught in the rain. It was a trifling cold, no more, but she's developed a fever and has not awoken in two days. Astrid doesn't request my return—in fact she bids me to remain where I am and promises to write if there's a change—but I feel I must go.'

Aunt Bea rose and came to squeeze Cressida's shoulder.

'It's too late in the day to set out, but we can leave at first light. Will that do?'

Cressida, worry lodged in her throat and tears in her eyes, only nodded, hoping the meagre movement could express all the gratitude she felt in that moment for Aunt Bea.

When the fine lady's coach pulled up in front of Blackbird Hall the following day, however, the only thing Cressida felt was concern for her sister, tinged with apprehension should she cross paths with her husband.

'Send a note should you need anything.'

'What will you say to him? Won't he think it odd you've returned so soon?'

'You leave him to me and turn your thoughts over to your sister.'

Cressida stepped away from the carriage so the footman could close the door and watched it only a second before turning towards the house. A footman directed her to the pink drawing room, the room where her aunt liked to compose her letters. It wasn't until she was wandering the silent halls that it occurred to Cressida how foolish she'd been. Cora wouldn't be in a sick bed in Blackbird Hall; she would be at Red Fern Grange. The frantic worry that had driven Cressida to take the impulsive trip was replaced with discontent. Either she would be forced to spend her days cooped up here awaiting news, which she could have done at a safer distance from Tamarix, or she would have to visit her childhood home and risk seeing her father for the first time since the confrontation in his study.

'Aunt?' The door to the pink salon was open, and Cressida saw her beloved aunt poised with pen in hand. Cressida's one word caused the poor woman to jump and smear ink across the paper.

'Heaven forfend, child! Are you trying to send me to an early grave?' Aunt Delia rushed from her chair, the letter no longer of any concern, to draw her niece up in her arms and kiss her head and face and head once more. 'Tell me you've returned for good.'

'I've come to see how Cora does. Astrid made it sound quite dire.' Cressida felt tears prick her eyes. Aunt Delia led her niece to a chair and took up the one near it, keeping Cressida's hand clasped in her own.

'It's not good, I'm afraid. The apothecary has very little hope, and although the physician down from London says all is not lost, he advises us to prepare for the worst, even as we continue to pray for her recovery.'

Cressida pulled in a tremulous breath. 'What's being done?'

'Everything possible. Would you like to see her? I am happy to escort you.'

'It's why I came back,' she said, 'but I think I need to go on my own. I've spent too long cowering.'

'Are you sure?'

'I am. I'll go tomorrow after breakfast. It's unlikely he'll even realise I'm in the house. In the meantime, perhaps you could quietly mention to the staff that I am...' She stalled. '... Just an apparition?'

Her aunt smiled, but Cressida thought it was a rather sad one. 'You won't stay? You won't see him while you're here?'

'I came for Cora.'

Aunt Delia looked as if she had much more to say, but she nodded once instead and guided Cressida towards the stairs. They had a quiet dinner and retired early. Cressida had brought along the book Mrs Peregrine had recommended, but she kept thinking of the one she'd left behind on her bed at

Tamarix and wishing she had not done so in a fit of pettishness.

The following morning, she boarded her aunt's carriage to Red Fern Grange. Despite the way things stood with her husband, she could never forget his defence of her in her child-hood home, and she wore that memory like a suit of armour.

Her breathing was more even than she'd expected as she knocked on the door of the Grange and greeted the house-keeper, who looked more than a little surprised to see her.

'Miss! I mean, my lady,' stuttered Mrs Hutchins.

Cressida offered her a tight smile. She found she did not miss the woman at all. 'Cora?'

The housekeeper nodded, 'Of course, of course. Come along. She sleeps still, but I believe the other girls are with her.' Mrs Hutchins opened the door to Cora's room, and two pairs of eyes grew wide, the owners of each springing to their feet to ambush Cressida.

She submitted to her sisters' embraces, every second they kept their arms around her further dissolving her resolve to stay away.

Astrid pulled back first. 'Whatever are you doing here?'

'This,' responded Cressida, with a small laugh to relieve some of the tension she'd felt coiling up inside her.

'You know what I mean.'

'This,' Cressida said again. 'Seeing Cora, tending to my sisters.' She reached out a hand to each of their cheeks before moving to Cora's side. Her sister looked so peaceful, as if she'd already found some other, better place to go to than the one where her body remained. It split Cressida in two. 'How is she? Truly?'

Rebecca sighed and shrugged. 'The apothecary has a dim view, and although the physician's isn't much better, he encourages us to read to her and speak to her, to hold her hand so she may feel our presence.' Her voice quivered, and she reached into her sleeve to retrieve a handkerchief.

Cressida picked up Cora's hand, placing a light kiss on it. 'Hello, dearest. I've missed you desperately. All of you,' she added, in a gravelly whisper. It wasn't just the weeks she'd been away. Since the night she became engaged, she'd felt distracted, often as if she was just a spectator in her own life, existing outside her body and watching herself go through each day. Then she'd married and he'd left, and she could think of nothing else at all.

'Perhaps we ought to take some air,' Astrid suggested.

'No, I'm all right. I don't want to leave her just yet.' Cressida missed how both her sisters peeked at the clock on the table.

'A quarter of an hour. You've spent too much time in a carriage.' With unusual determination, Astrid rose, pulling Cressida with her and steering her by the elbow from the room, Rebecca trailing in their wake.

They walked a little way from the house without saying anything until Astrid broke the silence that had, to Cressida at least, begun to feel strained.

'Aunt Delia speaks of returning to town when Cora's well.'

'Does she?' Cressida couldn't recall her saying so.

'She misses life in a bustling city, I think,' Rebecca added, and, after a pause, said with a touch of asperity, 'It's too bad she was unable to find one of us an eligible husband.'

Cressida replied, with a cross look at her youngest sister, 'I have an eligible husband.'

An unladylike snort came from Rebecca, and she persisted, despite the eldest shushing her. 'Aunt Delia is going to leave, and we'll be exactly where we started, which I find ridiculous, given we've now a marchioness for a sister. You don't care for him much, and for that I am sorry, but what's done is done and it's time to make the best of it. You punish us as much as him with your current behaviour—and since when did you become so chickenhearted? By the by, if you won't see him, you ought to at least send round a thank-you note.'

Cressida felt the familiar pricking behind her eyes. What her sister said stung, not the least for the truth of it all. She'd had no choice but to marry Lord Windmere. She had also been able to admit that doing so would position her to help her sisters. But in her darkest hours, she'd thought of no one but herself—what she felt, how she would live the life that was now hers. She hadn't once considered how her actions would affect anyone but herself and Lucius. Because her marriage, her relationship with him, regardless of why or how it began, had at some point become the most important thing to her. That knowledge came upon her with such force, she gasped for want of air.

A full minute passed before she recalled something else her sister had said. 'Thank-you note for what?'

Astrid answered when it became clear Rebecca had no more to say. 'Your husband is the one who sent for the physician.'

Cressida tilted her head in wonder and confusion. 'Lucius sent for him?'

At that moment, the man himself was walking towards the house, accompanied by a person who, judging by his attire and the bag in his hand, could only be the physician. Cressida was out of his line of sight and watched as he clipped past the short gate at the front and made his way to the door.

'He's been coming daily.' Astrid was as calm as Cressida was agitated.

Cressida couldn't take her eyes off her husband's tall, broad form. He raised his hand as if to knock but brought it back down. He looked once at the physician, then turned to glance over his right shoulder. His eyes didn't even need to search to find hers.

Cressida looked between her sisters and her husband in bewilderment. She felt rooted in the ground, unable to move or speak or even think a clear thought, but when Lucius looked in her direction, his face too far for her to tell what he felt when his eyes fell upon her, she turned, picked up her skirts, and ran.

There were no cries of shock behind her back, no shouts of her name, and no words pleading for her to stop. Or maybe there were, but she couldn't hear them over her own panting. She hadn't run this hard since she was a child and, despite the burning in her lungs and her legs and a stitch in her side that felt like it would rip her in half, she didn't stop until she'd reached the tidy little woods set at a distance from the property and was certain no one followed. From where she'd stopped, she couldn't see the front of the house, but she could see if someone was coming from that direction.

Her heart dropped a little when the only thing to come near her was a dove. She hadn't wanted Lucius to follow her.

Or maybe she had. She hardly knew anymore.

---

28

*L*ucius stood on the stoop of Red Fern Grange watching his wife run from him—too shocked by her presence to move, to call out, to do anything other than watch her go. The experience was one he'd rather not repeat.

'I'm sorry.'

He waved off Astrid's apology, shook the physician's hand and, without going inside, left as if the last few minutes hadn't happened. As his wits returned, all he could think about was how his wife's reaction when she saw him was to flee in the other direction at startling speed. She couldn't even tolerate the sight of him.

It crossed his mind to seek her out in the woods she'd run to, or else to ride to Blackbird Hall, where he supposed she must be staying, and wait for her return, but she'd not come back for him, and he would not force his attentions on her when she wanted only to spend time with her ailing sister.

He would not follow her. He would not wait at her aunt's

home. He would no longer call at the Grange. He would not frequent the village. He would not go beyond the boundaries of his own property while she remained near. For the first time in his life, Lucius Anselme would do nothing.

It proved harder than expected. As soon as he made the resolution, he wished to break it, to throw himself at her mercy, to beg for a chance he did not deserve. What he wouldn't give just to be in the same room as her once more, to make her smile, to hear her laugh, to show her how integral she'd become to his future. By the time he was dismounting at Tamarix, he'd already decided to leave again. He could not stay while she remained. He could not live with her so close and know her always to be beyond his reach. This time, however, he would leave her a letter. One for her aunt as well, in case Cressida consigned his to the flames.

He would sort out some kind of life for her apart from him. She could remain at Tamarix, near her sisters, which would be all she wanted, he already knew, and he would set up at some great distance. He would contrive to be in town with her next spring if she wanted to bring out her sisters. She would not like that, but it would help smooth their entrance if she appeared with him, rather than without. His aunt could lend her countenance and protect her in his absence.

He grimaced.

Lucius had written to his aunt of Cressida's disappearance in the event his wife kept up a correspondence with the lady. Instead of replying, Aunt Bea had swept into Tamarix and promptly took him to task for what she'd read in the papers.

'Of course that poor girl is gone, and who,' she cried, punctuating her point with a hard jab to his chest, 'are you to think anything of such a move? Perhaps she simply acted by your example. I'm for the dower house. Your person is most displeasing at present.' She turned and left in the same quiet fury in which she'd arrived. Lucius had seen very little of her since. Tomorrow he would speak with her and begin the unwelcome task of ridding his wife of her husband.

29

*H*er husband had not followed her.

It was the refrain repeating in her mind, even after Astrid came out to beckon her back to the house. Cora had opened her eyes and managed a weak smile. The physician was confident she would heal. That joyful news should have occupied Cressida's mind, yet when she finally returned to Blackbird Hall much later, she still half expected, half hoped to hear Lucius's rich warm voice drifting from somewhere in the house. There was only her aunt, however, alone, with a book in hand. He knew she was here, and he had not come. Whatever he wanted from her was not, it seemed, what she wanted from him.

Everything crystallised in an instant.

She couldn't leave again without that book of poetry—it was the one tangible thing she had that ever suggested he'd held her in high regard and affection. But leave again she must. Tamarix was his home before it was hers, and there was too much to do there for him to be absent long. She could return to Branford for a short time while she found a suitable establishment for herself, and a companion, too. Her allowance was plenty generous enough for such a thing, and she imagined he might be willing to increase it, if it meant he could be rid of her. Cressida hated the idea of leaving her sisters and once more resolved to do for them whatever was within her power, but she couldn't live with the uncertainty of seeing him, of being rejected by him, of watching him live his life without her.

As their separation drew on, she'd come to realise they were each deeply flawed individuals. She had begun to think of a future for them that wasn't perfect, but where they learned together, grew together. That hope was at an end, and all she could dream of now was a day in which he occupied the lesser share of her thoughts.

Bent on her course, Cressida rose early the following morning and walked the three miles to Tamarix Hall. Lord Windmere was in the habit of riding out most mornings, and she prayed today dawned no different. She went to the main gate, and in her grey coat and dress of dark green felt she was able to remain out of sight in the trees that ran along the drive. The only nerve-racking moment of exposure was covering the expanse of ground from the end of the tree line to the front door. She considered as she crossed the wide-open space that perhaps her worry was for naught. It was entirely possible that if Lucius saw her, he'd simply turn the other way. The thought brought her spirits to a new low.

Yates suffered no small shock when he opened the door and found himself staring into the wan face of his mistress. He let loose an undignified exclamation as he ushered Cressida into the foyer, offering to take her coat.

'It's all right, Yates, thank you. I won't be long. I've only come to retrieve something I left behind. I can trust you to keep my presence to yourself, can I not?'

'Of course, m'lady.'

She was gone in a moment, her soft leather boots hardly making a sound on the marble of the great hall. She wended her way up the stairs that led to the family wing, thinking it was perhaps the last time she would come this way. Coming to a stop at the door to her room, she paused, took one resolute breath, and pushed into the finest room in which she'd ever laid her head. She had only meant to get the book and go, but she had been ill-prepared for the feelings that would overcome her as she stepped into her chambers, which were beautiful and feminine and warm, and had only just begun to feel like her own when she left.

She wandered to the looking-glass, hardly recognizing the drawn face that stared back, and fingered the elephant figurine her aunt had brought her from India. Aunt Delia had given one to each of the girls: Cressida's had emeralds for eyes, Astrid's diamonds, Cora's rubies, and Rebecca's sapphires. The ornament was heavy and just a little too big to fit comfortably in her hand, but this time she would take it with her.

As she turned towards the bed, her elbow bumped a candle holder she didn't remember ever seeing, much less placing in her room. It fell to the ground with a muffled thud that felt as loud as a gunshot in the silence. Cressida held her breath a moment, and when a dozen footmen didn't push through the door, she set it back and turned to the bed once more.

Her hands had begun to shake, and she felt certain the restraint holding her emotions together was very close to bursting. The book wasn't on the counterpane, and with a bewildered look around the room, she saw it on the little table near the window.

She picked it up, but as she tried to open the cover, she lost her hold on the elephant, which tumbled to the ground at her feet. She knelt to retrieve it, knowing she shouldn't linger, but the draw of the words—his words—was overpowering. For just a moment, in this place where they would never build a life together, she wanted to imagine otherwise. So she remained there, kneeling on the floor of what would soon be her former chambers.

With trembling movements, she opened the cover, only to find that the words now so familiar, so dear, to her, were obscured by a folded sheaf of paper. She cocked her head to one side, turning her lips down in a frown. Her brow wrinkled in confusion. She knew with certainty she had not tucked any paper into the seam of the book and unfolded it with a painful mixture of curiosity and foreboding darting through her.

The writing she recognised as her husband's immediately, his strong, sharp lettering forever etched in her mind. But the words. Her breath caught in her throat, and she choked on nothing more than air and emotion.

How do I love you, wife —
the divine beauty
of your body and soul?

Her hands shook with such violence she could hardly maintain her hold on the paper, and tears she hadn't realised had formed threatened to melt away the ink.

I love you as one loves
scarce, obscure kinds of things:
Fiercely, without knowing how,
or when, or where I began.

The words began to whirl and coil before her. She pressed the heel of her palm first to one eye then the other, but it was no use.

I love you as you are—
your body of things absolute,
flesh and bone,
legs and arms,
that wrapped me up
and allowed me to feel your love.

There was a point of clarity for Cressida then: Lucius had been sitting in her room, reading her book, writing *her* a love poem.

I love your mind of things abstract—
things I cannot pull close
but can hear and see and feel
because before we were here
in this life together,
we were split and scattered,
like fragments of a dream.
Your name, the only thing
I could ever remember.

She thought she heard the wind kick up then, but it was only her breathing, harsh and uneven, coming in gasps and heaves, filling the quiet of her room.

That is to say, I love you in this way—
then and now, and again and always,
because I know no other.

The more she read, the harder she wept, and by the end, her cry was little more than a low, long howl of pain. Her realisation and the infinitesimal bit of hope it sparked was more than she could bear, and instead of pulling herself from the floor when she'd finished reading the poem, she began again.

30

*L*ucius had ridden out to inspect some wood rot on the dock at the boathouse and was discussing repairs with Johnson when Thomas, the first footman, came barrelling towards him, arriving out of breath and with a light sheen of sweat glistening on his forehead.

'My lord,' the young man wheezed, gulping in fresh air, 'Yates sent me at once.'

The hair on Lucius's arms stood, thinking only one thing could merit such urgency—the condition of Cora Ambrose. 'Out with it!'

'Yates promised not to tell anyone that someone is at the house.'

Lucius looked at the footman like he'd grown an extra set of limbs. All concern for his new sister fled and in its place impatience and irritability.

'I prefer not to be spoken to in riddles, Thomas.'

The footman gave Lucius a look that was part entreaty, part doggedness.

'My lord.' The footman tilted his head a little and emphasised eye contact with Lucius. 'Yates cannot tell anyone, that *someone* is at Tamarix, in *someone's* room right now, but *someone* won't remain for long.'

This time, the significance of the statement was not lost on Lucius. 'Oh, dear God,' was all he said, as he ran to where Helios grazed. He had promised to stay away, but she was here, and he would regret it always if he didn't at least try for something, anything, everything.

Without waiting for a groom to reach him, when he arrived at the stable he dismounted and ran up the steps at the side of the house, two at a time. He kept up this frantic pace, turning down one corridor and then the next until he was halfway down the hall to her room, where he pulled himself to an abrupt stop, comprehending that if he went barging in on Cressida she was likely to flee, just as she had at the Grange.

He walked slowly the rest of the way, silently thanking the extravagant former marquess for carpeting the halls, and edged the door open, thinking the slight movement would catch her attention.

Her back was to him, and she seemed oblivious to his presence, so he leaned against the doorway and savoured the sight of his wife here in their home, knowing she didn't intend to remain and wondering how he could convince her otherwise.

As she reached for the book of poetry he'd left by the window, something else slipped from her grasp. A soft '*Oh*' drifted towards him. He waited for her to retrieve what it was, to turn towards him, but when she sunk to her knees, she remained there.

Lucius heard the distinct sound of pages rubbing together as the cover opened and everything stopped: his heart, his breath, his world. He knew she would see the words he'd written before their wedding—when for a wink of time it had felt like all might somehow, someday come right—but that was not what stalled him on the threshold. He heard her unfold the paper, knew the exact moment she realised what it was, who it was for, who it was from.

Lucius had written his wife the poem during an interminable sleepless night as the candles burned till they guttered. He wrote it because he could think of nothing else, because he owed her more than he could ever give, because he needed to feel connected to her someway, somehow.

He wanted to wait, he wanted her to come to him by her own choice, but the choked breathing, the bowing and shaking of her proud shoulders, the forlorn wail that pierced the silence, broke him.

He came to his knees on the plush carpet behind her, too scared to reach out, but the stiffening of her spine, the hitch in her breath, told him she knew someone was there. One minute passed after another and alarm reached a fever pitch inside him. When she eventually, haltingly, began to turn, he stopped breathing, his heart stopped beating, everything stopped except her.

Cressida brought her gaze to his. He hoped she could see his contrition, his longing. She clamped her eyes shut, her hands shooting up to cover her face. With gentle motions, he pried them away, so he could replace her hands with his own, one on each cheek. He waited, and when she didn't move, didn't run from his touch or the room, he pressed his lips first to her right eyelid and then to her left.

Another strained sob burst from her lips, and he traced them with the pad of his thumb before caressing her damp cheeks. He trailed airy kisses from one temple to the other, charting a course over her reddened nose.

Lucius stared at his wife, making a thousand silent prayers

and promises. Her eyes fluttered open, bloodshot and swollen and even more vivid in their unusual colour. They were also full of misery and uncertainty, and he berated himself for doing this to her. He pressed a kiss to her forehead before letting his own rest there. Her breath was uneven and hot on his mouth and chin. He brushed the tip of her nose with his own, living for nothing more than the exquisite closeness of her—as if the memory must carry him through his lonely years ahead.

He kissed her again, slow and lingering, on one corner of her mouth, then the other, and it was the work of an instant to capture her lips with his own in a featherlight kiss that lasted just long enough for him to taste the salt left behind from her tears. He snaked his arms around her body, crushing her to his chest, and buried his face in her neck, nuzzling the exposed flesh as his ragged breaths fluttered the strands of hair that had escaped their pins.

There was an acute stinging in his eyes when he felt her wrap one slim arm, then another, round his neck.

'Please don't go, my love. Please. Don't go.' Lucius waited for Cressida to say something, anything, and felt her take several deep breaths against his arm. When she at last spoke, the words were infinitely dear to his ears.

'I've missed you terribly, Lucius.'

He took her hands in his and dropped a kiss into each of her palms before pressing them to his face and revelling in the feeling of her soft, tender touch, the delicate lines she was tracing on his skin along his sharp cheekbones and sharper jawline. She ran her fingers over his lips, the bridge of his nose, his eyebrows. She combed through his hair, and chills prickled every inch of his skin. He closed his eyes and released a long exhale set free from some unknown place only she could touch.

If given the chance, he would have stayed wrapped up with her forever, but there were things he must say to her, things she deserved to hear. He opened his eyes, reclaimed her hands, and stated without preamble, 'There are no excuses for how I treated you on our wedding day or for leaving you after. I am sorry, Cressida. You deserve a man better than the one I have proven myself to be.'

'No.' Her head dipped. 'If I'd been honest with you—and how many opportunities I have had to do so—the entirety of the scene could have been prevented.'

'You want a portion of the blame, but I concede none. That another man ever laid claim to your heart filled me with a jealousy I had no right to feel.'

'Stop.' She interrupted with a bitterness of spirit that took him by surprise. 'I must tell you, before you say more, the whole truth of it.'

He had no wish to hear anything about her feelings towards another man but would not deny her anything she asked.

'James Heaston was good-looking, cordial, charming—until he wasn't. I never wished for his attention, much less sought it out. My lack of interest only seemed to make him more determined.' She told her husband how this man had come upon her once as she walked after breakfast and forced a kiss on her. She struggled but suspected the only thing that saved her from him that day was the fortuitous arrival of Sophia's eldest brother, who was home from school and came up with some pretence to escort her to the rectory.

A week or so after, the viscount had made a grab for her wrist as she passed by him in the village. She'd flung her hand away but landed a scratch on his face in the process. The final time she saw him, she was in the barn at the Grange checking on a litter of kittens. Astrid had gone to fetch some old linens, and Viscount Torring, finding Cressida alone and set on avenging himself, threw her down into the hay. She landed on something hard, and when he brought himself over her, she hit him square in the head with an old horseshoe. It dazed him enough that she was able to flee, nearly knocking into her sister as she ran. Together they watched him leave from a window on the first floor.

'On his ride home, he fell from his horse and broke his neck. Lady Lisle knew of his intention to call at the Grange and found me at fault for his accident.' She hesitated, before adding, 'And perhaps in some ways I was. If I had not hit him—'

'No. No!' The fury Lucius had felt at first was soon replaced by compassion for his wife and the litany of terrible things she'd been subjected to at the hands of others, himself not excluded. His stomach turned. He took her by the shoulders. 'Look at me, Cressida. The only person at fault is him.' Although she nodded, it was unconvincing, so he said nothing further but wrapped his arms around her and held her close until she pulled away and peered up at him. Something played in her eyes he couldn't quite make out.

'If you meant these words—' she began with a weak gesture towards the book on the floor near them.

'I did. I do.'

'Then how could you go to London and—and—' Cressida broke off, her skin reddening at the question she wanted to ask and couldn't. 'The papers. Lady Colchester. I know who she is.'

Lucius's stomach seized. He'd forgotten all about that

woman. 'Is that why you left?' She nodded and he discovered it was possible to feel even worse than before. 'I didn't, not what you think anyhow, but it's entirely my fault you've been labouring under such a heavy misapprehension. Had I been more circumspect, more thoughtful, when in town—' He took a deep breath, knowing the only way forward was to tell her the whole truth. 'You gave me honesty. I will do the same. We cannot begin anew with secrets or misunderstandings between us.'

Cressida gave an unsteady nod.

'First, you must know I've not lain with a woman since before I came to Tamarix.'

Her eyes searched his, and it took every muscle in his body not to look down in shame.

'But it was not long after returning to London that I thought to take up with my former mistress. I believed you to hate me, to want nothing to do with me. I convinced myself in order to assuage my own guilty conscience.' Lucius could see the hurt on her face as he spoke but pressed on. 'I was seen in company with her more often than I should have been, although nothing transpired between us until one night'—he swallowed hard—'she kissed me and I kissed her back, trying to convince myself that what I wanted wasn't back at Tamarix. When she touched me, I felt nothing but disgust for the man I was becoming, a man I didn't recognise and didn't like. I walked away from her then and never looked back.

'I'm ashamed to say it took that moment, some other woman's hands upon me, to realise the only person whose touch I long for is yours.' His voice split as he finished, and he rested his head on their intertwined hands.

She released a breath that had been lodged in her lungs. 'You didn't—you don't have a—a—'

'No. There is but one woman in all the world meant for me. I am yours, only and always, if you'll have me.' He paused, deliberated, and, feeling it was the last of many things for which he must atone, said before he could change his mind, 'I followed you into the library. I knew you'd gone in alone. I had no idea what I would say to you, only that I was profoundly affected by our dance, and I entered the room behind you before I could think better of it. Had I known Lady Lisle was watching...' He shook his head. 'This, all of it, is my fault.'

His wife was quiet for a very long time. 'I ought to be furious with you, but the truth is you were a danger to me long before that night, from the second I turned in Mr Taff's bookshop and saw you—how I clung to that moment. But when I discovered who you were, how close you'd be, I wanted to despise you because I knew I could never be with you. You see, I had long believed I could never be with anybody, let alone a titled gentleman, because how could I let someone commit to a life with me without revealing that I may be the natural daughter of an unknown man, and how could I trust someone enough to say as much otherwise? It was a secret I refused to keep from my husband, and a secret I saw no way of revealing.'

'You told me.'

'In a fit of temper,' she said, with an uneven smile, 'and I thought you'd withdraw your suit. Why didn't you?'

'Because I was already more than half in love with you.'

She pinked and looked down at their hands, his large fingers woven with her smaller ones. 'I should never have gone to Branford Park. For better or worse, that's what I vowed, and when it was worse, I ran away, ignoring the hypocrisy of my own actions.'

'Branford?'

'Yes, with Aunt Bea.'

'You've been at *Branford* this entire time?'

She laughed and looked a little embarrassed. 'Yes. It's even more charming than you said.'

Lucius was both amused and a little upset, but not with her. 'The choice words I have for my aunt and brother. I was driven to distraction by your disappearance!' Indeed, his waistcoats were a little loose, the hollows of his cheeks more pronounced, and every letter he'd written while she was gone was merely a collection of nonsensical phrases strung together.

'Don't be cross with them. It was unbearable to remain here alone, thinking about you being with another woman in town, thinking you thought so little of me, of our marriage. It was selfish and unkind of you to go off like that, but I have been selfish and unkind, too.' She said the words without condemnation, which made him feel the error of his ways all the more.

'No. The mistakes have all been mine. I forced you into this marriage and left you here laid bare. Had I learned earlier to consider your feelings as I ought—as you deserve—had I thought of *you* instead of myself, perhaps all this could have been avoided.'

'Oh, Lucius, we have both been more foolish than we have the right to be.'

'We are all fools in love, but we are the lucky ones to have the rest of our lives to learn to do better. For now—' He ended his sentence by pulling his wife onto his lap and kissing her soundly.

'Lucius?' She said his name tentatively as her hand came up to run along the stubble on his cheek and chin.

'Yes, my love?' he asked, between sprinkling kisses on her nose and cheeks and forehead. She didn't answer right away, and when he felt her shift her weight, he pulled back to make sure nothing was amiss. 'Cressida?'

Her flushed cheeks went a shade darker. 'Will you—will you make me your wife?'

His brow pulled down. 'You are my wife.'

'No. Yes. That is, on paper.' She tripped over her words and struggled to maintain eye contact as she spoke.

Lucius was about to ask what she meant, when the weight of her words settled in his chest and his eyes went wide. 'Now?'

She nodded, and he nearly tossed her off his lap as he went to lock her door.

Cressida came to a standing position, her eyes never leaving his person as he made his way back to her. Without a second thought, he swept her off her feet and into his arms, savouring the feel of her before depositing her at the edge of the bed. She looked at him, confusion settling over her delicate features.

'Turn around.'

She did as he bid, and when her back was to him, he began to undo the long row of buttons on her dress until he could slide the sleeves from her shoulders. His fingers stroked the curve of her neck, the top of her back, the swell of her chest. She shuddered, and he pushed the fabric down her arms and continued past her waist, putting out his hand for her to hold as she stepped from the puddle of sprigged muslin.

Lucius released the tie of her petticoat and loosened her stays, wishing he had his penknife so he might just cut through all the laces. When all that remained between him and her body was her shift, he gathered the fabric in his hands and wordlessly pulled it over her head. The sight of her brought him to his knees.

'Sit.'

Cressida sank onto the bed, and Lucius took one of her feet, setting it upon his knee. His hands worked upwards to the creamy white skin of her thigh and, with aching slowness, he rolled her stocking down. Her other leg was given the same treatment, and when she was fully, completely bare before him, he set about kissing every inch of her exposed skin. He began at her ankle, teased the backs of her knees, met the exquisite taut flesh of her thighs with his tongue.

'Lie back.'

He took her hips in his hands and brought her forward so her centre was near the edge of the bed. When his mouth closed around her and his tongue flicked the little pearl under her curls, Cressida let loose a frantic gasp and made to push herself up.

'Lucius.'

'Did you not like that, dear one?'

Her eyelids fluttered rapidly as if trying to make sense of both the action and her reaction. 'No. it's not that. It's just—it felt—I didn't realise—and your mouth—'

While she spoke, he brought a finger up, tracing her folds with a featherlight touch. She watched his hand, but he watched her, mesmerised by the expressions of pleasure and interest playing across her face and the ready response of her body.

He paused only long enough to rid himself of his own clothing. His hardness jerked when his wife studied it, her eyes darkening with understanding and desire. Lucius thought he saw trepidation, too. 'We'll go as slow as you like.' She acknowledged his words by settling herself fully on the bed and making a space for him.

Lucius sank down next to her, forcing himself to go slower

than his taut, throbbing body desired. He had nearly ruined everything; he would not ruin this. He brought his hand up to cup her cheek, his thumb idly stroking her bottom lip. 'I love you, Cressida.'

She smiled against his finger. 'And I you—then and now, and again and always.'

ACKNOWLEDGMENTS

I like to think this book would have come to life one way or another, but I don't know if that would be true without my husband, Keola, whose absolute and endless support allowed me to hole up in my snuggery and chase a dream.

This book is for the teachers who inspired and supported my lifelong love of reading and writing and who I've thought about often on this journey, especially Zoanne Richardson, Helen Copeland, Sydney Brown, and John Gery. And for my fellow writers, workshoppers, and castle wine drinkers.

Thank you to my editors, Joanna Hinsey and Sarah Pesce, my proofreader Helena Fairfax, and my cover designer Robin Vuchnich for their collective efforts that turned a jumble of words on a page into a real book.

To my family and friends who championed me from the very beginning, thank you—for believing, for manifesting, for being my biggest cheerleaders.

Once again, thank you to Joanna, who had the dubious pleasure of living in my brain during this process and whose insight, advice, and encouragement I'd be lost without.

And thank you, dear reader. I am so grateful and so humbled that you chose to share your time with me.